Night of the Chupacabras

NIGHT OF THE CHUPACABRAS

Marie G. Lee

AVON CAMELOT

AVON BOOKS, INC.
1350 Avenue of the Americas
New York, New York 10019

Copyright © 1998 by Marie G. Lee
Interior design by Kellan Peck
Visit our website at **http://www.AvonBooks.com**
ISBN: 0-380-97706-0

Library of Congress Cataloging in Publication Data:

Lee, Marie G.
Night of the chupacabras / Marie G. Lee.
p.   cm. — (An Avon Camelot book)
Summary: When Mi-Sun and her younger brother spend the summer in Mexico with their friend Lupe, they become convinced that there is a mysterious vampire-like monster killing Tío Héctor's goats.
[1. Mystery and detective stories. 2. Mexico—Fiction.
3. Mexican Americans—Fiction. 4. Korean Americans—Fiction.
5. Ranch life—Mexico—Fiction. 6. Uncles—Fiction.] I. Title.
PZ7.L5138Ni   1998   98-7996
[Fic]—dc21   CIP
                            AC

First Avon Camelot Printing: October 1998

CAMELOT TRADEMARK REG. U.S. PAT. OFF. AND IN OTHER COUNTRIES, MARCA REGISTRADA,
HECHO EN U.S.A.

Printed in the U.S.A.

FIRST EDITION

QPM   10   9   8   7   6   5   4   3   2   1

For my two mothers:
Mamá Jacoby
and
O-Ma Lee

School's Out!

RIIIIInng! The last school bell sounded, and the students streamed out of Public School 33 like a pack of birds being set free into the sky.

Mi-Sun Kim flowed along with the tide of kids in sneakers, shorts, and strangely light backpacks. She had made it through sixth grade—junior high was next! It seemed almost unbelievable. Mi-Sun remembered entering P.S. 33 as a scared first grader, and now she'd graduated with almost perfect marks—including "best attendance." She was still a little afraid of what junior high would bring— harder classes, all those big kids, the *huge* school building— but that was a whole summer away.

Summer!

"Hey, Mi Sol!" It was Mi-Sun's best friend, Guadalupe García, otherwise known as Lupe. Lupe had come to her school when Mi-Sun was in third grade. They had become friends and gone through P.S. 33 with all the same teachers. Now they were done with crabby old Mrs. Reich, their sixth grade teacher, who had announced on the first day of school that she didn't want to hear *one* word of a foreign language in the classroom even though, for instance, Mei-tien had just come from China and Janna spoke Russian only at home and both girls needed friends to translate for them at times. Lupe spoke English fine, but she liked to play with words, like calling Mi-Sun "Mi Sol," which meant "my sun" in Spanish. Get it?

"So, have you asked your parents yet?" Lupe inquired, her greeny-brown eyes large and hopeful.

"No, I haven't," Mi-Sun admitted.

"But *chica,* I'm leaving in a week."

"I know, I'm sorry—I just don't know how to ask them."

Lupe was going to spend June and July with her uncle, Tío Héctor, in Mexico. He said Lupe could bring a friend, so Lupe naturally asked Mi-Sun. Mi-Sun was excited. Mexico! She had never been.

But how to ask her parents? They expected her to spend her summers helping her mother in her store, and she had plenty of unofficial duties, like taking care of her younger brother.

"And they'll probably want me to go to *hakwon,* summer school," Mi-Sun went on. "They're afraid I'm going to forget my Korean, and also I need some help in math."

"Mi Sol," Lupe said firmly, "how are your parents supposed to know about this great opportunity if you don't tell them? Mexico will be *better* than summer school. You'll learn all sorts of new things, including Spanish."

Mi-Sun thought for a second. "Lupe, why don't you come to dinner? I'll ask them, but you can back me up."

"Sure," said Lupe. "Just let me use the phone to call *mi mamá.*"

When the girls arrived at the Kims' apartment, Mi-Sun's baby brother, Ju-Won, was lying on the couch in his usual state: reading a horror novel. Their parents weren't home yet.

"Nuna," he said, which means "older sister." "We're supposed to get the vegetables ready for dinner." He reburied his face in *There's a Killer in Bunk Nine: Welcome to Camp Cannibal.*

"Okay," Mi-Sun said, putting her and Lupe's bags in her room. Their mother and father both worked, so Mi-Sun and her brother were used to helping with dinner.

Mi-Sun managed to separate Ju-Won from his book, and set him to removing the stringy tails from a pile of bean sprouts. She started chopping celery while Lupe tackled the red pepper. Mi-Sun cut diagonally, like her mother did, so the pieces would come out in pretty crescent moons. Lupe, on the other hand, handled the knife like a surgeon, slicing the pepper into precise, neat squares. As they worked, the two girls continued the conversation they'd begun at lunch: cute boys at school and which music groups they thought were the best.

Mi-Sun and Lupe had always liked "unplugged" singers who played the guitar and sang simply, but this year, Lupe had started listening to groups that used lots of special effects and sang loud, crashy music. Lupe's parents, in the meantime, were always trying to get her to listen to Mexican folk music, which Lupe dismissed as "hokey."

Mi-Sun looked over and noted that Ju-Won had cleaned a grand total of three bean sprouts—enough dinner for a grasshopper. He was sitting there, looking up, as if he were a friendly dog waiting for someone to notice him.

"Hurry it up, Ju-Won," Mi-Sun said. "At this rate we won't be eating those sprouts until next year."

"It's hard work," Ju-Won whined. "The tails are so stringy. Why don't you help me?"

"Don't pull your *agi* act on me," Mi-Sun warned. Ju-Won had just finished third grade, but he often acted so childish that the family had started to call him "agi," which means baby in Korean.

"And I don't think New Blue is a very good group, either," he said. "They sound like frogs."

"Quit eavesdropping into our conversation," Mi-Sun said, annoyed.

"Wow, Ju-Won has even heard of New Blue?" Lupe said with awe. "I don't think my little brother has, and he's older than Ju-Won."

"Agi-face sneaks into my room and listens to the CD," Mi-Sun explained. "I don't think he can tell the difference between a good group and a bunch of burpy frogs, either."

Mrs. Kim came home first. She and her friend, Mrs. Park, owned Han-Mi Grocers, which carried food as well as a little bit of everything else: Hello Kitty pencil cases, special candles with Jesus or the Virgin Mary on them, scented cardboard cutouts that cab drivers liked to hang on their rearview mirrors. The strangest thing they sold were the "good fortune" sprays, which were supposed to bring the user luck. They had specific ones for money, love, and happiness. She and Lupe had tried them—all three at once—but they didn't do anything but make Lupe's room smell like old strawberries.

"Oh, hello, Lupe," said Mrs. Kim. "I didn't see you behind that huge pile of vegetables."

"Anyonghaseo," said Lupe. Mi-Sun had taught her how to say "hello, how are you?" in Korean and bow.

"O-Ma, can Lupe stay for dinner? She cut up that whole pile of peppers."

"Of course," Mrs. Kim said. She set a bag of groceries on the counter. "Tonight we're going to have *jap-chae* to celebrate the end of school."

"Hurray!" said Mi-Sun and Ju-Won. Jap-chae, glass noodles and vegetables, was one of their favorite dishes, up there with pizza from Pepe's, the pizza parlor next to Han-Mi Grocers. Mrs. Kim put on her apron and said they could watch TV.

"Watch TV?" Mi-Sun repeated, confused. Usually, after her chores were finished, she would have to rush to do her homework. Then Mi-Sun remembered she didn't have any homework. The free time felt almost strange.

As soon as Dr. Kim arrived home from Queens Hospital, they sat down to eat. Mi-Sun's mouth watered at the sight of vegetables glistening with noodles and meat and the big pile of spicy Korean pickles, *kimchi.*

As they began eating, Dr. Kim asked the children about their last day of school. He was big on education and always reminded Mi-Sun and Ju-Won how hard he had studied to get into medical school in Korea. Mi-Sun was thinking she might like to be a doctor, too—a veterinarian, actually—so she studied hard.

"Mine was fun—we sailed paper airplanes when the teacher had her back turned!" said Ju-Won. When he saw the disapproving looks on his parents' faces, he added quickly, "It was just a sub, anyway. She didn't know any of our names."

"How was yours, Mi-Sun?" Mrs. Kim asked.

"It was okay," Mi-Sun said slowly.

Lupe kicked her under the table.

"Um, and Lupe invited me for a, uh, summer adventure."

"A what?" asked Mrs. Kim.

Mi-Sun swallowed. All of a sudden, a summer in Mexico seemed immense. Mi-Sun didn't even know if she could ask her parents for such a thing.

Lupe kicked her again.

"Lupe is going to visit her Uncle Héctor in Mexico for June and July, and he said she could bring a friend. Can I go?" Mi-Sun rushed her words out as fast as she could, almost hoping her parents wouldn't be able to hear them.

There was silence at the table. Even Ju-Won stopped stirring his jap-chae noodles with his chopsticks.

"It would be a great way for Mi Sol, I mean Mi-Sun, to learn Spanish," Lupe piped up.

Mi-Sun's mother cleared her throat. Mi-Sun thought she saw a big "N-O" forming in her mouth, but instead, Mrs. Kim asked, "Mi-Sun, you've never been away for that long—how do you feel about it?"

"Fine," Mi-Sun said. "I really want to go."

Dr. Kim turned to Lupe. "What does your uncle do?"

"He's a rancher. He has a goat ranch in a small town called Tierralinda. It's in Sonora, a state on the U.S. border."

"Are you sure it's okay with him?"

"Oh sure. I was there two years ago, and Uncle felt bad because he doesn't have any children, and there aren't any near the ranch. I didn't mind too much— I read a lot of books. But this time he wants me to have company. He said I could bring one or even two friends."

"I don't know," Mrs. Kim said, switching to Korean. *"I was hoping you would be starting hakwon this summer, Mi-Sun. And it would be good for you to help me at the store."*

"But this would be better than summer school!" said Mi-Sun in English. "I'd be learning Spanish in Mexico—and think of how helpful that would be."

Mrs. Kim's brow furrowed. She couldn't deny that knowing Spanish would certainly come in handy in the store. Mi-Sun knew enough Korean to talk to Korean customers, but most customers who didn't know English spoke Spanish. Their Queens neighborhood was home to Mexicans, Dominicans, Colombians, Ecuadoreans and Puerto Ricans, and it wasn't a coincidence that the store carried tortillas and guava and yucca root as well as apples and Spaghetti-Os.

"It's very generous of your uncle," Mrs. Kim said.

"Oh no," said Lupe. "He would *like* having us around, I guarantee it."

"But what about Ju-Won?" Dr. Kim asked.

"He can take care of himself," said Mi-Sun.

"No I can't," Ju-Won said. "I'm only in third grade."

"Quit being such an agi—you're technically in fourth grade," said Mi-Sun.

"Children!" said Mrs. Kim.

"Hm, that is a problem, Mi-Sun," said Dr. Kim. "What about your little brother? He can't stay alone in the apartment all summer."

Mi-Sun rolled her eyes. Leave it to Ju-Won to get in the way of *this,* like he did with everything else.

"I know!" Lupe said suddenly. "Why doesn't Ju-Won come to Mexico with us?"

"Hm," said Dr. Kim.

"I don't know if that would be an imposition on Lupe's uncle," Mrs. Kim said to her husband.

"Oh no," said Lupe. "It's totally fine with him—the more the merrier. Really. He has a huge house."

"Ugh," said Mi-Sun. "I don't want agi to come with us. He'll whine the whole time and be a bother."

"And I don't want to go to Mexico, either," said Ju-Won, wrinkling his nose as if he smelled sour milk.

But suddenly, Mi-Sun realized there was no way her parents would let her go if Ju-Won didn't come, too. Silently agreeing with her, Lupe kicked her under the table for the third time.

"Ju-Won, I was just kidding," Mi-Sun said. "I would *love* for you to come along—and think of how educational this trip will be."

"Who cares?" said Ju-Won. "I'd rather stay in New York where it's safe. I bet they have zombies or something in Mexico."

Only Mi-Sun knew the depth of her little brother's addiction to horror novels. He checked garbage-bags-full of them out of the library, so many that the librarian once gently suggested he "leave a few for the other children." At home, he would read them after school as well as late into the night, under the covers with a flashlight. Mi-Sun worried that he had scrambled his brain with so many gross images that he was beginning to think these bizarre stories were real.

"Agi, zombies don't exist except in your head," she said scornfully. "And besides, when's the last time you read about a zombie that speaks Spanish?"

Ju-Won sat back in his chair and stuck out his lower lip. Mi-Sun knew from experience that he could hold that pose for hours.

"Hey, Mi-Sun," Lupe said now. "Don't you think it'll be more fun if it's just us? My tío's ranch has so much fun stuff to do. For instance, we can get slingshots at the *mercado* and learn how to shoot them."

"Really?" said Ju-Won. He'd only seen slingshots in

cartoons. He imagined having a slingshot and learning to shoot a whole row of cans. Ping! Ping! Ping! Wouldn't his friends be impressed?

"And my uncle has this cook, Consuela," Lupe went on. "She makes the best *tamales*. Consuela looks like a star from a Mexican soap opera, and she's fun, too. She knows lots of games and once she showed me how to make soap. But—ooh—those tamales. *¡Delicioso!*"

Mi-Sun knew that Ju-Won would be drooling just thinking about tamales, a mixture of cornmeal, pork, and cheese all baked in their own little cornhusks and topped with spicy sauce. They had first tried them at Lupe's house for *Cinco de Mayo,* the Mexican celebration day on May Fifth. Ju-Won had practically never stopped thinking about them ever since. It was smart of Lupe to get at him through his stomach.

"Hm, maybe Mexico could be kind of fun," he mumbled.

"Yeah," Lupe said, grinning wickedly. "If it's just me and Mi-Sun, there'll be more tamales for us. And just think—down in Mexico they eat them *all the time,* not just at Christmas and Cinco de Mayo, like we do here!"

"I want to go!" Ju-Won exploded.

This time, Mi-Sun kicked Lupe under the table. Lupe just smiled. Later, she would complain that Mi-Sun had bruised her shin.

"I'll call your parents and start making arrangements," Mrs. Kim said.

Destination: Mexico

The next week, the families took two taxis to the airport. Mi-Sun and Lupe were so excited, they couldn't stop chattering. At the airport, they ran to the windows in the departure lounge and watched the planes come in. Mi-Sun had arrived on a plane from Korea when she was four, but she didn't remember much of it, so she considered this to be her first real airplane flight.

At the check-in, their parents talked to the flight attendants, who promised to make sure the three of them got on their connecting flight.

When it was time to board, Ju-Won looked as if he was being sent off to Timbuktu to eat yak butter for the rest of his life.

"Be a good boy and mind your big sister and Lupe's

Uncle Héctor," Mrs. Kim said, hugging him. Ju-Won didn't look up. His lower lip looked like it could reach back to their apartment in Queens.

"Don't worry, he'll be good," said Mi-Sun. "I'll make sure of it." She itched to get on the plane and begin her trip.

But when her mother gave her a long hug, Mi-Sun found herself feeling sad. She suddenly realized she wasn't going to see her *omoni* and *abogee* for two whole months!

She looked over at Lupe and her parents, and saw that Lupe, too, looked unhappy.

A voice called their flight over the loudspeaker. "Final boarding call, all passengers should be on board."

"Let's go!" Mi-Sun said bravely.

"*¡Vámonos!*" said Lupe, taking her hand. Mi-Sun took Ju-Won's hand, and tugged gently. Ju-Won was holding tightly to his father's hand, and Mi-Sun felt like she was peeling a banana as she coaxed him toward her. Ju-Won held on for as long as he could and let go only at the last second.

"Goodbye," said both sets of parents. "Goodbye."

The three intrepid travelers made their way down a long tunnel into the body of the plane.

Ju-Won let some tears fall as he looked out the plane's window. "I miss O-Ma and Ah-Pa," he sniffled. "I bet Mexico is going to be scary.

"Agi, what would there be to be scared of in Mexico?"

"Scorpions and snakes and bears and stuff."

Mi-Sun was surprised he didn't add Ju-Won-eating aliens, zombies, and bloodsucking vampires to his list.

Mi-Sun knew there were scorpions in Mexico because she had seen Lupe's: it was tiny, but with a clearly visible stinger, preserved in a clear plastic paperweight that said RECUERDO DE MEXICO. When they were studying arachnids, the spider family, in school, Lupe had brought it to show the class. She had almost given Mrs. Reich a heart attack—Lupe had to convince her the thing wasn't alive. Mi-Sun resisted the urge to tell Ju-Won about that.

"Here, read your book," she said, handing him one of his favorite *Scream Street* books that she'd brought for an emergency. Out of all the different kinds of books available, Ju-Won read only two kinds: sci-fi and horror. Mi-Sun thought his sci-fi kick was understandable—she liked Madeleine L'Engle herself—but she had no idea why he was so wild about horror books. This one was called *Massacre at the Funtime Arcade*. The cover had a picture of two hairy fists holding a bloody ax with assorted severed limbs sprawled next to some video games. Yech.

After the plane took off, Lupe opened the box her mother had given her. Inside was *pan dulce*, sweet, soft bread fresh from the neighborhood *panadería*.

"Look, pan dulce!" she said. "Ju-Won, look." She handed him the biggest one, and he happily stuffed his face as the rest of his tears dried. Then, while Lupe and Mi-Sun chatted excitedly about the summer ahead, Ju-Won not only finished *Massacre at the Fun-time Arcade,* but he also started another book, *Vampire from Outer Space,* which he unpacked from his carry-on.

"Wow," he said. "Sci-fi *and* horror. I'm in heaven!"

Tierralinda

In Arizona, they changed planes and took a smaller Air Mexico plane to Ciudad Obregón, where Tío Héctor would meet them and drive them to Tierralinda.

"Ay! Ay! Ay!" cried a mustachioed man in a straw cowboy hat when he saw them get off the plane.

"That's Tío Héctor," Lupe said, waving.

The man ran up to them excitedly.

"*Son mis amigos, Mi-Sun y Ju-Won,*" Lupe said, by way of introduction.

"*Ay, mucho gusto,*" nice to meet you, said Tío Héctor.

He took them out to a giant pickup truck and hoisted their heavy suitcases in the back. His arms looked like they were made from heavy rope.

"Can I ride in the back?" asked Ju-Won. Lupe translated the question. Her uncle said something, shaking his head slightly.

"Sorry," Lupe said. "We have a way to go, and Tío said it's too dangerous."

Ju-Won put on his long agi-face, but Tío Héctor seemed not to notice. He helped them into the cab of the truck.

The ride took them along winding roads that seemed to lead nowhere. Mi-Sun didn't see many houses, or stores, or much of anything. Just bare deserty ground. As the sun started to set, long shadows seemed to reach at them, like snakes.

"I-I-I don't like this place," Ju-Won said. "It gives me the creeps."

Tío Héctor looked at them questioningly.

"Ju-Won dice que es muy diferente de la ciudad de Nueva York," Lupe translated for her uncle.

"I told him it's a big change from the big city of New York," she said to Mi-Sun.

"You should be a diplomat," replied Mi-Sun.

Suddenly, Ju-Won sat bolt upright.

"L-o-o-o-k!" he yelled. "A headless monster!"

Mi-Sun looked where Ju-Won was pointing. She felt her heart jump into her throat—a headless thing was waving at them!

The Monster Who Waves

SCREECH! Tío Héctor stomped on the brakes and said something to Lupe, looking at Ju-Won with concern.

"Está bien," Lupe answered, which Mi-Sun knew meant "fine."

"Mi-Sun," Lupe said to her. "Tío thinks Ju-Won needs a doctor! I told him he's just scared of everything."

"Help!" yelled Ju-Won, covering his eyes and kicking his legs. "It's going to get us—Tío Héctor, what are you doing?"

Tío Héctor looked outside and chuckled.

"You think ghost?" he said. He pointed calmly at the headless thing. Ju-Won's eyes were covered so tightly by his hands it looked like you'd need pliers to pry them off.

Mi-Sun followed Tío's finger. "Oh," she said, looking more closely at the man-sized figure. "It's a cactus."

"Saguaro cactus," said Tío Héctor.

"I've heard other people say they look like people, too," Lupe added, kindly.

"But Ju-Won, you're the first to make so much noise seeing one," Mi-Sun grumbled, jabbing her brother with her elbow. "Look, Agi, it's just a cactus."

Ju-Won cautiously lifted one finger and peeked out. "How was I to know?" he said. "We don't have cactusseses in Queens."

"Cacti or cactuses," corrected Mi-Sun. In the shadows, the cactus did look a little like a headless person waving at them. But it was clearly just a plant. In fact, one of its "arms" had a hole in which some birds were nesting. Mi-Sun could see them flitting in and out and twittering.

"*¿Está bien?*" Tío Héctor asked. His mustache twitched, as if something inside him wanted to keep chuckling.

"Tío wants to know if you're okay," said Lupe.

"I'm o-okay," Ju-Won said reluctantly. "I don't know if I like Mexico, though."

A little while later, Tío Héctor made a turn next to a big sign on a fence that said RANCHO DE CABRAS.

"*Cabras* are goats," said Lupe. "Tío raises them, as well as chickens and stuff, but mostly goats. Maaa."

As they bumped up the long dirt road that was the driveway, Mi-Sun could hear barking in the distance, coming closer. Tío Héctor must have dogs! She loved all animals, but especially dogs.

Then a dog that looked to be part German shepherd came bounding down the lane. It woofed happily as it ran alongside the truck.

"*Es nuestro perro, Tuki,*" Tío Héctor said. As soon at the truck stopped, Mi-Sun jumped out to pet her. She had the black snout and bushy tail of a German shepherd, but her ears flopped in a way that made her look friendly and intelligent at the same time.

"She's so cute!" Mi-Sun exclaimed, scratching her behind the ears. Tuki smiled, showing nice white teeth. No one in Queens had such a big dog. Mostly, people had tiny yappy dogs that they could squish easily into an apartment.

As Mi-Sun petted Tuki, her eye caught a movement in the clay-colored house. It was dusk, but she could make out a woman standing in the doorway, squat as a statue and dressed all in black.

"Lupe, who's that?" Mi-Sun said, pointing.

"Where?" said Lupe, looking. "There's no one there."

Mi-Sun looked again.

The woman was gone, as if she'd just silently detached herself from the shadows around the door.

Then they heard an unearthly cry.

Perros

It took Mi-Sun a second to realize the scream came from Ju-Won. Right by his feet, a mangy-looking dog with liver-colored spots had somehow crept up and begun attacking Tuki. The liver-spot dog made a scary growling sound in its throat as it leapt at Tuki. Tuki snapped back, and the animals turned into one furry whirlwind as they spun and thrashed, barking and yipping and yowling.

"Ay! Ay! Ay!" yelled Tío Héctor, grabbing a shovel that leaned against a tree. Mi-Sun feared he was going to start whapping the dogs with it, but instead he just waved it around, yelling something in Spanish.

"*¡Fuera! ¡Lárgate, maldito perro!*"

20

Lupe ran into the house. She came out with a bucket of water and soaked both dogs. The other dog broke away, yipping as it ran down the driveway. It was so thin that Mi-Sun could see its ribs, and it was missing one of its ears.

"Es un diablo," muttered Tío Héctor. A devil.

"Did Tuki bite that dog's ear off?" Mi-Sun said, the yowls still ringing in her own ears.

"Oh no," said Lupe, bending down to pet Tuki and search her for injuries. "That other dog is—how do you say it, not tame?" Even though Lupe had been in America almost as long as Mi-Sun, she spoke Spanish at home, not English, as Mi-Sun did with her parents. Every so often, she would forget an English word.

"Wild," said Ju-Won, who seemed to have found his tongue for the first time.

"Sí, wild," said Lupe. "His ear has been like that since I can remember. We call him *Una Oreja,* One Ear. He's always fighting."

"Why doesn't someone bring him to the pound or something?" said Ju-Won, who wasn't particularly fond of dogs.

"Oh, that *loco* thing belongs to a man in town. The dog's name is *Muñeca,* doll. Such a pretty name for such a mean dog."

Tío Héctor wiped the sweat off his face and then motioned everyone to go inside. Mi-Sun realized that she was very, very hungry. She followed Lupe into the house. Its knobby sand-colored walls looked like they'd been made out of clay, or plaster. Inside, it was nice and cool, and Mi-Sun caught a glimpse of an orchard in the back. Lupe led them to the dining room, where plates of enchiladas and tortillas and salsa sat before them on a wooden table.

"Yum," said Ju-Won. "I'm starving!"

La Downtown

Mi-Sun and Lupe woke promptly at eight o'clock the next morning. But maybe because of all the excitement the night before, Ju-Won did not get out of bed even when the sun, *el sol,* was high in the sky.

"Ju-Won sure likes to sleep," remarked Lupe.

"I guess he's pooped," said Mi-Sun as she shoveled the last of the tortillas, eggs, salsa, and beans into her mouth. Mexican food was like Korean food, she decided: spicy and best eaten mooshed together.

"That was yum," said Mi-Sun. "But where's Consuela?" Once again, there had been a meal waiting for them, but no trace of the cook.

"I don't know," said Lupe.

23

"It's weird she didn't come out to say hi to us. Last time I was here, we had so much fun together! I think you'll like her. Maybe she'll show us how to make tamales."

"I think I saw her last night," said Mi-Sun. "Isn't she kind of old and dresses in black?"

Lupe gave her a look.

"Mi Sol, Consuela was eighteen years old last time I was here. And she likes rainbow colors and mini-skirts the best. I don't think I *ever* saw her in black—only widows wear black."

"Well then, who was it I saw?"

Lupe shrugged. "A vampire?"

"From outer space?" Mi-Sun added.

They both laughed, thinking of Ju-Won.

"What are we going to do today?" Mi-Sun asked.

"First, the dishes, since Consuela doesn't seem to be around," said Lupe. "Then we'll go to *el centro*—I call it la downtown—to see the sights, and Tío asked me to pick up a few things."

Mi-Sun already loved the Rancho de Cabras, partly because there were so many animals. Chickens and pigs ran all over, looking as if they might even barge into the house. The goats grazed in the field along the orchard next to the cows and floppy-eared burros. Tuki sat under the shady tree in the front yard and kept an alert eye on everything.

When Ju-Won finally woke up and finished break-fast, they all went into town.

* * *

"My feet hurt," complained Ju-Won after they had gone barely three feet down the dirt driveway.

"Ha jee ma," Mi-Sun said in Korean, so she'd sound just like their mother. "Stop it. Quit being such a city kid. What do you want to do, take a subway?"

Mi-Sun noticed that Ju-Won was wearing his oxfords, his good shoes from the day before. She would have asked why he didn't wear his sneakers, but his face was stretching into his I-won't-talk-to-you-and-I'll-pretend-not-to-even-hear-you pout, so she knew not to bother.

The driveway led to a winding road. They walked past more houses all made of the same bumpy material as the rancho's house. Mi-Sun stopped to feel the bumps with her fingers.

"That's *adobe,* clay made out of sun-dried earth and straw," Lupe informed her. "Almost all the houses here are made of that. It's good for this climate, and it keeps the house really cool."

"See, isn't that clever?" Mi-Sun said to Ju-Won. "Adobe. You learn something every day."

Ju-Won made a face. "Basically, Lupe is saying the house we're staying in is made out of mud," he said.

Mi-Sun rolled her eyes. This was going to be a long summer!

Beware!

The downtown of Tierralinda was charming. It had all sorts of small stores and offices, and the three of them wandered into a park with shady trees, a little gazebo, and benches for sitting.

"This is the *zócalo,* the center of town," explained Lupe. "In a Mexican town like this, all roads lead to the zócalo, so if you want to see someone, you just come here and wait. Eventually, you'll run into them—I guarantee it."

Lupe led them to the row of stores next to the zócalo. There was a feed store, a fabric store, a shoe store piled high with leather sandals.

"Let's go in here," said Lupe, pointing to an open doorway.

The sign outside said TIENDA.

26

It was a general store, filled with food, toys, hardware supplies, dishes, and other sundries, just like Han-Mi Grocers.

A man behind the counter was counting out some eggs for a lady. When he looked up and saw Lupe, he smiled. He spoke in rapid Spanish to the lady and helped her bundle the eggs up into a big cloth.

"Que le vaya bien," he called as she walked out of the store.

"Hola, mija," he greeted Lupe, and he kept talking. Mi-Sun gathered they were talking about school and the United States. Lupe bought a bag of flour that said MASA on it. After the man wrapped it up for her, he got down a plastic jar labeled CHUPAS. He opened the top and pushed it across the counter toward them. It was full of lollipops.

"He said the treat's on him," said Lupe. "He's a friend of Tío's."

They each took one.

"Gracias," they all said on the way out.

"Yug," said Ju-Won as he sucked on his candy. "What the heck flavor is this?"

"Tamarind," said Lupe, as she enthusiastically bit hers. *"¡Delicioso!"*

"What the heck is a tamareen?"

"It's a fruit, I think. Oh, maybe it's a vegetable. It comes in this brown pod, like beans."

"Brown pods like poop," said Ju-Won. "It makes me want to throw up."

"Ju-Won, be nice," said Mi-Sun, who wasn't that crazy about the sweetish, syrupy flavor, either. "It was nice of that man to give you a free candy."

"ACCCKKKkkk." Ju-Won made a huge gagging noise. Both girls looked down to see a glistening pool of barf with the candy floating on top!

"I told you it made me want to barf," Ju-Won said, grinning in a strange way.

"Should we go back to the tienda and get you some Pepto-Bismol?" asked Lupe, trying not to look too disgusted.

Mi-Sun gingerly kicked at the pool of barf. It didn't move. She kicked it again. It was plastic! She picked it up and threw it at Ju-Won, who was laughing hysterically.

"Where'd you get that?" said Lupe, unable to stop up her own giggles. When Ju-Won did stuff like that, Mi-Sun wanted to kill him. But Lupe would laugh, which only encouraged him.

"I got it as a bonus with *Attack of the Slime Ejectors*," he explained. "It sure fooled you, didn't it?"

Lupe admired the plastic barf for a moment. "Oh," she said, handing it back to him. "We have to go back to the tienda anyway. I forgot to get lime for the tortillas."

"You're making sour tortillas?" said Ju-Won.

"No, lime is this white powder you put in with the cornmeal to make it soft." Lupe turned around and started back toward the store.

Outside the tienda, an old man on a folding lawn chair dozed happily under the shade of his broad-brimmed straw hat. While Lupe went inside the store, Mi-Sun and Ju-Won waited beside the chair.

The man's left eye opened. It was brown. Then his

right, which was a bright, shining, blue. He seemed to stare at nothing, and Mi-Sun wondered if he was blind.

"*Hola,*" said Mi-Sun hesitantly.

"*Hola, mijos,*" he said. His mouth opened to a smile that was missing several teeth. He pushed up his hat and got a good look at the two of them. "*¿Chinas?*" he asked.

Mi-Sun shook her head. She knew that much Spanish: "*No, coreanos,*" she said. "*Norteamericanos,*" she added.

He said something else in Spanish that went by her, like a train she'd missed. "*No sé,*" she said. She had reached the end of the line with her Spanish.

"What your names?" he said in English, to their surprise.

"Mi-Sun," she said. He smiled his gappy smile again.

"*Como sol,*" he laughed.

"That's what Lupe calls me," she told him, nodding in the direction Lupe had gone.

"Where did you learn English?" Ju-Won wanted to know.

"I work," he said, proudly pointing a finger upward. "In *el norte,* picking fruit. Many year, Florida."

"Florida isn't in the north, it's south," said Ju-Won.

"North of *here,* Einstein," said Mi-Sun. Ju-Won ignored her.

"I'm Ju-Won," he said.

"Juan?" said the old man. His breath whistled a little between his teeth. "Name is Juan?"

Mi-Sun laughed.

"Yes, it's Ju-Won," she said, pronouncing it the Spanish way, like "wan." She patted him on the shoulder. "Ju-Won-ito—our little Juan."

"Where live in Tierralinda?" he asked.

Mi-Sun tried to remember the name she saw on the ranch sign. Rancho de . . . Rancho de . . .

". . . Rancho de Cabras," she finally remembered. She remembered the word only because it had "bras" in it.

"Ay," said the man, rocking forward slightly. His brown and blue eyes both darkened like storm clouds. "*Peligroso*. Beware. Beware, CHUPACABRAS!"

Paletas

Just then, Lupe returned with a small bag.

"Hey, look!" she said suddenly, looking across the zócalo and pointing. "The *paleta* man. This is going to be the best part of the whole summer—follow me." She began running, so Mi-Sun and Ju-Won followed, leaving the old man behind.

The three of them clustered around a young man pushing a cart. Even though he was wearing a huge shady sombrero, his face was the color of kimchi with lots of red pepper. He probably stayed in the sun for a long time every day.

He was selling paletas, huge popsicles. He had an amazing array of flavors scrawled on his hand-lettered sign: *piña, limón, melón, coco, tamarindo, guayaba, mango,* and *tuna*.

"Tuna?" said Ju-Won, making a face. "Is it the whole fish on a stick or do they take it from the can?"

"It's not tuna the fish," said Lupe. "Tuna is the fruit of a *nopal* cactus."

"Maybe he has barf flavor, Ju-Won," Mi-Sun said helpfully, pointing at the sign. "Smooth or chunky, just like Ben & Jerry's."

Juan made another face, sticking out his tongue, which was still stained brown from the tamarind. "I'll take pineapple."

"*Una de piña,*" Lupe instructed the paleta man.

Mi-Sun carefully avoided the tamarind and got a lime one, which she ordered herself: "*Una de limón, por favor.*"

Lupe got a coco, and she gave the man some pesos.

"Gracias," he said, smiling as he squinted into the sun.

They sat on one of the pretty white benches and ate their paletas. For something that *looked* like a plain old popsicle, paletas were something else. Mi-Sun thought each lick felt like she was taking a bite of a cold, delightfully sweet lime. Even better, the paleta was filled with juicy pulp. Normal popsicles just tasted like water, juice, and sugar.

Back at the tienda, the old man and the chair had vanished.

"Who was that man outside the tienda?" Mi-Sun asked Lupe.

"The *abuelo?* I don't know. He was kind of weird," Lupe said. "I don't remember meeting him before."

"He came up with a great Mexican name for me," said Ju-Won. "Juan."

"Juan, Ju-Won. I like that."

"By the way, what does 'peligroso' mean?" Mi-Sun asked.

"Dangerous," Lupe said.

Mi-Sun gulped. "You know, the old man, the abuelo, when we told him where we lived, he said 'peligroso.' "

"He thought our house was dangerous?" Lupe said with a frown.

"I don't know," Mi-Sun said. "He said beware of something called a chupacabra."

"Chupa cabra?" said Lupe. "Goat sucker? Are you sure you heard right?"

"I think that's what he said. I know he said cabra, and I remember the word 'chupa' from those suckers the guy at the tienda gave us."

"Ay," Lupe sighed. "Either you're hearing wrong, or that abuelo is telling you a story."

"But he said 'dangerous,' " Ju-Won insisted, looking worriedly at his melting paleta.

"I think that abuelo was probably sitting out in the sun too long and cooked his brain—what would he know about Tío's ranch?" said Lupe.

Mi-Sun decided Lupe was probably right, the old man was yanking their chain. Lupe's grandmother, her *abuela,* made up stories, too. Once she had even told them that her eyeball fell out when someone accidentally knocked her on the back. She had made the whole thing into a vivid story, recounting how the eyeball was attached to her head with this stuff that looked like fine white string. How weird her eye socket felt without the eye in it. How she had a *curandera,* a folk healer, pop it back in for her, using chants and sacrificing a chicken. With all those details, ironically, the story seemed almost real. That was the point, Mi-Sun supposed.

Mi-Sun looked over at Ju-Won.

"Peligroso," he mouthed to her when Lupe had her back turned. "Dangerous."

Night Noises

As Mi-Sun was getting ready for bed, Ju-Won barged into her room.

"I don't like this place," he said. "It's so far away from everything that no one can hear us if we scream."

"Ay," said Mi-Sun. She liked how that word sounded, like sighing out loud. "What on earth is there to scream about?"

"Remember what that abuelo was telling us about, that abracadabra thing?"

"Chupacabra," she corrected. "Abuelo means grandpa, in case you didn't get that. He's just a grandpa having a little fun with you."

"He seemed pretty serious to me."

35

"He was just spinning a yarn to give pesky little kids nightmares. Lupe's abuela does that all the time. Once, she tried to tell us her eyeball had fallen out of her head. Go to sleep, Ju-Won."

"Can I sleep in here with you?"

"Look, Tío Héctor cleared out that whole room so you could have a room to yourself."

"I don't want to be by myself."

"Agi, you've got to quit reading those *Scream Street* books. O-Ma keeps telling you they give you nightmares. You'll get so tired, *you'll* end up looking like a zombie and scare the pants off the rest of us."

"That has nothing to do with *Scream Street*—this place is scary all on its own."

"If this place is so scary, why does Tío Héctor live here? How come we don't see severed limbs all over the place like in *Massacre at the Funtime Arcade?*"

"How do we know he *really* is Tío Héctor? Maybe he's some kind of alien who *looks* human, but he's going to drink our blood first chance he gets. Lupe is his accomplice who tricks us into coming down here—don't you remember how excited she was when I said I'd come too? Remember?! More food for old vampire Tío!"

"Ay," Mi-Sun said again. "Once an agi, always an agi. If it makes you feel better, I'll sit in your room until you fall asleep. But I tell you, there's nothing to be scared about."

Just then, the two of them heard a clicking noise coming from the hall. It came closer and closer, sounding like some giant insect gnashing its teeth.

Click-CLICK click-CLICK!

"Help!" Ju-Won whimpered as he clutched at Mi-Sun. She found herself desperately clutching him back. "Get Tío Héctor!" she whispered. But neither of them could move.

Click-CLICK click-CLICK!! It was very close now. Suddenly, the door swung open.

Claws

"Aieeee!" they yelled. "Aieeee!"

They heard the sounds of struggling, running, a voice shouting "Ay! Ay! Ay!"

Too late, Mi-Sun saw that the clicking sounds came from Tuki, who'd nosed her way into their room. The dog looked curiously around her.

"*¿Qué pasó? ¿Qué pasó?*" shouted Tío Héctor, tripping over Tuki in his haste to get into the room.

Mi-Sun started to say something, but her throat was completely dry and closed like a sealed envelope. It took three swallows to get it to open up. Tuki had really scared her!

"*Perdón,*" she said. "Tuki scared us."

"Monster," Ju-Won whimpered.

38

Tío Héctor slumped down. He looked at Ju-Won, then at Tuki—who wagged her tail—and then he laughed.

"*Mijo*," he said to Ju-Won. "*Tuki no es un monstruo.*"

"I know," Ju-Won said quietly. "We *thought* it was a monster. He was clicking."

Lupe, rubbing her eyes, appeared in the doorway. "What the heck's going on?"

Mi-Sun felt the red claws of embarrassment on her face. She could imagine how O-Ma and Ah-Pa would scold them if they were here! It was their first full day in Mexico, and already they were causing trouble for their host's family!

"Sorry, Lupe," she said. "We're just not used to hearing Tuki move around—she was making funny clicking noises. We don't exactly keep large dogs in our apartment in Queens."

"What did you *think* it was?" Lupe laughed. "Dogs have claws that click on the floor; they can't pull them in like cats do."

"Well," said Mi-Sun. "You learn something new every day."

Tuki got up from where she was sitting and clicked her way over to Ju-Won. She put her head forward to be petted, but he didn't touch her.

Tío Héctor yawned. "Sleep," he said. "Ah—" He bent down and picked up one of Mi-Sun's sneakers and shook it. "*Cada día*—every day, do," he said. "*Alacranes—peligrosos.*"

"See!" said Ju-Won. "He said 'peligroso.' There *is* something to be scared about!"

"Ju-Wonito," said Lupe. "Tío just said to shake out your shoes every morning before you put them on, to make sure there aren't any scorpions in them."

"S-s-s-c-orpions?" said Ju-Won.

"Yes, we have scorpions down here."

"I don't like this," Ju-Won whined. "You aren't supposed to have scorpions down here!"

"Come on, Ju-Won, scorpions have to live somewhere," said Lupe. "Tío was just saying you should do that as a precaution. Scorpions like shoes because they're nice and dark, so you just have to give them a chance to get out. You wouldn't like it if you were sleeping and some big ugly foot came in and kicked you, either."

"I'm scared," said Ju-Won.

Mi-Sun looked down at her sneakers. It made her feel a teeny bit ill to contemplate the possibility of a scorpion curled up in there. But she decided she had to be brave to show Ju-Won.

"Ju-Won," she said. "The little scorpion is probably scareder of you and your stinky feet than you are of him."

Lupe yawned. "Ju-Won and Mi-Sun, don't scream so loud next time, okay? I need my beauty sleep."

When Lupe and Tío Héctor left, Mi-Sun felt like scolding Ju-Won, but she was too tired. She went with him into his room, as she had promised, Tuki following behind them. She was surprised that Tuki didn't feel rejected by Ju-Won, but instead lay down by his bed as if she were protecting him. Ju-Won fell asleep almost as soon as his head hit the pillow.

"Figures," Mi-Sun thought to herself. She smoothed his blanket and went back to her room.

Mi-Sun snuggled into her bed, which was covered with a bright Mexican blanket to keep her warm during the surprisingly cool night. Far off somewhere, a rooster crowed (didn't it have a watch?), but otherwise, it was very, very quiet. In Queens, she could always hear cars and buses going by, voices talking on the street, no matter how late it was. Out here, the quietness made her feel alone. She had no idea she would miss the sounds of Queens.

Lady in Black

The next day, el sol was up bright and early, as usual, and so was Mi-Sun.

"Any more nightmares about Tuki?" Lupe joked as they met outside Mi-Sun's room.

"Ha-ha, very funny," said Mi-Sun.

In the kitchen, a woman was roasting a chile pepper over the gas flame. She was all in black, which seemed out of place in the brightness of the Rancho. She didn't turn around when Mi-Sun and Lupe came in, but kept roasting the pepper.

"Buenos días," Lupe said, remembering her manners. Good morning.

The woman muttered something in reply, but still didn't turn around. On the table were bowls of yogurt and granola as well as chopped-up fruit.

Lupe didn't make a move toward the food, so Mi-Sun stayed behind her.

"¿Dónde está Consuela?" Lupe asked.

The woman waved the chile pepper over the fire.

"En México," she said. The pepper blistered and shriveled. *"En la universidad."*

Lupe's face fell.

"I guess Consuela went away to college in Mexico City," she told Mi-Sun. "This lady must be Tío's new cook."

"I think she's the one I saw the day we came in," Mi-Sun said.

The woman's name was María. That's all the two girls found out about her. When asked where she lived, if she had children—two questions that would set the average Tierralinda resident to cheerful explanation—María gave them a look that seemed set in stone, so they didn't ask her anything more. They ate their breakfast without speaking. It seemed weird to talk with María there.

Ju-Won still wasn't up, so while the morning air was fresh, the two girls decided to go downtown.

"I bet you didn't know that Tierralinda is also a good place to shop." Lupe grinned as she led Mi-Sun into a store that said ZAPATERÍA AZTECA. Inside, shoes and boots sat in a display case—but in the middle of the store was a big bin of sandals, the kind that Lupe and everyone else in Tierralinda wore.

"A present for you," Lupe said as she dug through a pile until she came up with a pair her size.

Mi-Sun tried them on. They were a simple basket-weave leather stapled to heavy rubber soles. Mi-Sun thought they looked a little strange, but they were nice and cool. Even sneakers felt hot in this humid weather.

"They are called *huaraches*," Lupe explained, and she turned them over and pointed to the soles. "See the nice thick rubber? They're made from old tires. Talk about recycling, huh?"

Mi-Sun nodded. She walked around a little. Ah, air-conditioned feet.

Mi-Sun wanted to see more of el centro, so Lupe took her all the way to the other side, where they could smell a wonderful smell of fresh bread.

The sign outside the store said PANADERÍA. Through the window, they could see breads and cookies piled high in bins, and people picking them out with huge tongs.

"Wow," said Mi-Sun. "This is exactly like the one in Queens!"

"Nope, the one in Queens is exactly like the one *here*," corrected Lupe.

They went inside and gazed at all the goodies that were being taken out of the oven and dumped, steaming, into the bins.

"Let's get some pan dulce for your tío to make up for the big scare we gave him last night," Mi-Sun said, scooping up a few and putting them on a tray.

Luckily, Mi-Sun's parents had given her an advance on her allowance.

"Okay. Here, these are good, too," said Lupe, picking up some white cookies. "These are *hojarascas*, Mexican sugar cookies."

At the checkout, Mi-Sun pulled out her wallet. The clerk punched in some numbers at the cash register, and it rang up $6,000.

"Six thousand dollars?" Mi-Sun gasped.

Lupe laughed.

"It's in pesos, silly," she said. "This is an old-fashioned register—there aren't so many zeroes in Mexican money any more."

"Oh," Mi-Sun said. She had forgotten they used different money here.

"I'll pay for it," said Lupe as she put a few coins on the tray. "We can go to the *casa de cambio* later to change your money."

When they got home, they put the panadería bag on the table, where Tío Héctor would see it when he came in. There was no trace of María, but they could hear the clumping sound of Ju-Won coming into the kitchen.

"Where were you guys?" he said, his voice teetering on a whine.

"Downtown," said Mi-Sun. "Look, Lupe found me these sandals—aren't they cool? Nice and airy, and they're made out of old tires."

Ju-Won stared at Mi-Sun's new shoes.

"I need a pair, too," he said. "I didn't bring my sneakers—I only have my good shoes."

"Agi," Mi-Sun said sternly. "If you want some hua-raches, fine, we'll bring you to the zapatería later, but don't lie. I saw O-Ma pack your sneakers in your suitcase."

Ju-Won pushed his lower lip out in a pout.

"I'm not lying, Nuna," he said, kicking at the floor with his heavy oxfords. "I took them out."

"You took them out?"

He nodded. "I wanted to have more room for my *Scream Street* books. I was afraid that while you and Lupe were running around all over the place—like this morning—I'd be stuck with nothing to do."

"Ay, we weren't abandoning you," Mi-Sun explained. "We just thought we'd get some stuff done while you were still in bed."

"I still want some hoo-racheeze. In fact, there's another good reason I need them," he said, his voice still sounding whiny and babyish.

"Why's that?" said Lupe.

"So I can see if there are any scorpions waiting to ambush my feet."

"Ay," said both Mi-Sun and Lupe.

The front door banged, and Tío Héctor came in, looking tired. He slumped down at the table like a balloon losing air. Tuki came in, too, and sat at his feet.

"*¿Qué pasó, Tío?*" Mi-Sun asked.

"*Una de las cabras, la madre con la cría,*" he said. "*Salió por un hoyo en la barda anoche. No puedo encontrarla.*"

Lupe looked sad. "He said the mama goat—the one with the kid—is missing."

"What happened to it?" said Ju-Won.

"It got out during the night, I guess." Lupe shrugged.

"Through the fence?" said Ju-Won. "How'd the goat manage to do that?"

"Probably there was a hole in the fence or something," Lupe said.

"Uh-oh," whispered Ju-Won. "Sounds like it might be the work of the abracadabra monster."

"Chupacabra," Mi-Sun corrected.

"*Qué es?*" said Tío Héctor.

"Oh, *nada*," Mi-Sun said quickly—no need to remind Lupe's uncle of how they'd woken up the whole house last night because of Ju-Won's overactive imagination.

They waited until the shadows were a little longer to return to town. Besides, at lunchtime, the storekeepers changed their ABIERTO signs to CERRADO, and closed their stores to eat lunch and take a siesta.

"If we get you these huaraches, you better wear them," warned Mi-Sun as they walked.

"Okay, okay," said Ju-Won.

They went into the Zapatería Azteca to search for huaraches in Ju-Won's size, but he was much pickier: he wanted the soles to be very black, and not too worn down, with zigzaggy treads.

"Okay, so you want us to find Goodyear All-Season Radials from the winter of 1996?" Mi-Sun grumbled as she pawed through the pile. Her hands were turning black from the tires.

Finally, they found a pair that Ju-Won liked, although they looked identical to the fifteen other pairs he had tried on. Mi-Sun paid, and they left the store. Outside, the abuelo was sitting in his usual chair front of the tienda, slurping a paleta.

"Let's ask him about that chupa thing that kidnapped the goat!" Ju-Won cried.

"Oh please," said Mi-Sun.

"Hola," said the abuelo, looking their way. "You saw chupacabra?"

"No, no, we didn't see anything," said Mi-Sun.

"There's this missing goat, a mother goat with a kid, actually," Ju-Won explained, speaking a mile a minute. "We think it's been kidnapped. Tío Héctor can't find it anywhere."

"Did you get all that?" said Mi-Sun doubtfully.

"*Claro,*" said the abuelo. "Chupacabra steal goat, suck blood out of goat, make it dead." He made loud slurping noises on his paleta.

"What does a chupacabra look like?" Ju-Won wanted to know.

"Ay," said the abuelo. "*Muy feo.* Ugly, ugly. Red eyes, sharp things like *espinas* all over. And these things—" He flapped his arms.

"Wings?" said Ju-Won.

"Sí, wings. You have *papel?*"

Lupe looked dubious, but she pulled some paper and a pen out of her backpack.

"*Bueno,*" said Abuelo as he began to draw on the

paper. He drew with quick, sure strokes. The three of them craned their necks to see.

"That thing looks like the Grinch!" Ju-Won said, pointing at the drawing. "It looks like a vampire Grinch with spines of a *Jurassic Park* dinosaur all over him—and folding wings like a bat."

That was a pretty good description, Mi-Sun thought. The chupacabras, according to the abuelo, looked like a cross between a vampire Dr. Seuss character and a dinosaur. It also had wings, but walked with its "arms" jutting forward like Frankenstein. Mi-Sun had to admit the abuelo had a pretty good imagination; he and Ju-Won must read the same horror books.

"Have *you* seen a chupacabra?" she asked him.

"Sí, sí," said Abuelo. "Once, at night. It made dogs bark—dogs very sensitive to chupacabras. Next day, many dead goats."

"See! See!" said Ju-Won. "It's real. The chupawhatever probably broke through the fence and stole that goat and ate it, like fast food, you know? Cheaper than McDonald's."

Mi-Sun tried not to roll her eyes. She needed to take those *Scream Street* books of Ju-Won's and throw them out the window.

"Hey, Ju-Won," Lupe said, to distract him. "Want a paleta?"

"Sure," he said. "I always have room for one." Visions of fruit-filled paletas crowded out pictures of goat-eating chupacabras in his brain as they walked across the zócalo.

"Now, what flavor should I get today?" he said.

"Try tuna," Mi-Sun teased.

"Nah," he said. "I liked the one you had last time—what was it?"

"Lime," she said, and turned to the vendor. *"Dos de limón, por favor."*

"Y una de coco," added Lupe.

They ate their paletas as they walked back to el rancho, and they were licking the last fruit pulp from the sticks when they came into the yard. María was hanging up some clothes on a line.

"Buenas tardes," said Lupe.

"Buenas tardes," Mi-Sun and Ju-Won copied her.

María looked for a second as though she might smile or cry—and that her face would crack if she did either. She nodded as they passed, but didn't say anything.

"She doesn't like us, does she?" said Ju-Won as they walked into the house.

Tuki entered the room, wagging her tail. Lupe petted her and Mi-Sun gave her a hug. But Ju-Won edged away.

"What have you got against Tuki?" asked Lupe as Mi-Sun called Tuki to her. She had burrs stuck in her coat, and Mi-Sun began picking them out.

"Dogs scare me," Ju-Won said. "Especially big dogs like that. Did you see him fighting the other day? Does Tuki mean 'fang' in Spanish?"

"Tuki doesn't mean anything—it's a name," said Lupe.

"And Tuki's a she," said Mi-Sun, working out a particularly stuck burr. Tuki whimpered as Mi-Sun gently yanked at the fur, but she pawed the ground and wagged her tail to let Mi-Sun know it was all right.

"Tuki only fights when she has to," Lupe said. "She guards the house."

"She's still scary."

"Ay, you are such an agi," said Mi-Sun as she stroked Tuki's now burr-free coat. Tuki panted and smiled at her. "Besides, didn't you hear the abuelo? He said dogs are very sensitive to chupacabras, so here you have your very own live chupacabra detector."

"Fang," said Ju-Won.

In the evening, a tamale feast appeared on the table. Tío Héctor was still roving the ranch and would be late for dinner. Lupe invited María to join them, but she just shook her head and disappeared.

"Wow, these are good," said Ju-Won, peeling the cornhusk from another tamale. Next to his plate, the used husks were piled up like autumn leaves. "These are almost as good as your mom's, Lupe."

"I know," said Lupe. "Don't tell her that, though. Mamá thinks she has no competition. Anyway, we only have them once or twice a year. They're a lot of work to make."

After supper, they went to the zócalo. Girls in colorful flowery dresses sat on the park benches. Young men in cars and pickup trucks cruised by slowly, calling to the girls, who kept their eyes on the ground, but sometimes just barely blushed and smiled.

"Are they going anywhere, or are they just going to drive around the park a zillion times?" asked Ju-Won.

"People like to drive around and around, showing off their cars," said Lupe. "Lots of them go up to el Norte, make some money, and the first thing they buy is some big truck. And then they go around and around and around . . ."

"Oh, Tío Héctor should show off his truck," suggested Ju-Won.

"Tío is too busy for stuff like that," Lupe said. "And he needs that big truck to tend to all the *animales*."

"That would be funny, though," said Mi-Sun as she watched the cars drive by, blasting music. It wasn't the salsa she'd heard on the streets in Queens. It was more like country music with guitars that still sounded Mexican, like the stuff Lupe's parents were always trying to get her to listen to.

A truck went by with a load of young men in the back. They waved at the people in the zócalo as if they were in a parade. Mi-Sun smiled. Sometimes, she still couldn't believe she was in Mexico!

It was very dark when they returned to the ranch.

"Hm, we have company," said Lupe. A group of men including Lupe's uncle were clustered, talking, in the yard and pointing to something on the ground. They were so preoccupied that they didn't notice the children. Mi-Sun, Lupe, and Ju-Won crept into their circle to see what the men were looking at.

A goat was lying on the ground.

Mi-Sun looked more closely. The goat's eyes were

shut tightly, as if it were sleeping, but it also had two bloody holes, right in its neck! She knew that the poor thing was dead.

Dead!

"Wow, did you *see* that?" said Ju-Won when he came into Mi-Sun's room later. "That goat had *vampire* toothmarks on it! Now, if that isn't the chupacadabra thing, it's definitely some other kind of vampire."

"I'm sure there's an explanation for it," Mi-Sun said, but she was a little unsettled, too. She hoped she wasn't catching the Ju-Won disease that would cause her imagination to run away with her. She didn't want to find herself screeching in fright at the sight of a cactus.

"This is *just* like *The Vampire from Outer Space*, as a matter of fact," Ju-Won continued. "In that story, no one knew what was going on for the longest time— that's how the vampire was able to ambush so many people and suck their blood."

"Tell you what," Mi-Sun said to her brother. "If you can give up your *Scream Street* books for something real to read—here, how about this book about a girl who wins the Iditarod dog sled race in Alaska?—I'll supply you with paletas every day."

"I don't want to read about any yucky girl—or any *estúpido* dogs," Ju-Won said in his full-agi mode. "Besides, the paletas only cost one peso. My advance on my allowance should allow me to buy at least sixty paletas."

"Fine, have it your way," Mi-Sun sighed. "Don't blame me if you have nightmares."

But that night, Mi-Sun was woken up by something, and it wasn't Ju-Won.

Shadows in the Yard

Tuki was barking her head off.

Mi-Sun ran to the window. Because there was no moon, it was completely dark outside.

There was a rustling sound somewhere in the yard. Mi-Sun stiffened. She wanted to run to Tío Héctor's room and wake him up, but she couldn't tear herself away from the window.

She squinted hard.

A big shadowy thing moved past her window, the way a fish moves through dark water.

It was walking on two legs.

Mi-Sun didn't even know she had screamed.

But all of a sudden, people came running.

55

"Ay! Ay! Mija!" exclaimed Tío Héctor. He was followed by Ju-Won and Lupe.

"A thing . . . a thing, out in the yard . . ." was all Mi-Sun could say. Tío Héctor ran out, taking Tuki with him. In a minute, she heard Tuki outside, barking.

"Are you okay?" said Lupe, sitting with Mi-Sun on the bed. "What happened?"

"I saw something," Mi-Sun said, gathering her breath. "There was something walking in the yard. I don't know. Tuki must have seen it or smelled it, too."

"The monster," Ju-Won said, his eyes widening.

For once, Mi-Sun was inclined to agree with him. Whatever had been out in the yard wasn't meant to be out in the yard—and it hadn't looked human, either.

Tío Héctor came back in.

"Nada," he said, scratching his head.

"Nada?" said Mi-Sun.

He said something to Lupe.

"He said everything looks fine," Lupe said. "Tuki might just be barking at a *jabalina,* a wild pig, or something."

"Does he think we're crazy?" Mi-Sun whispered to Lupe. Lupe shook her head.

"No," Lupe said. "He didn't say anything like that at all. Honest."

Mi-Sun looked up at Tío Héctor.

"Perdóname," she said. "Lupe, would you please tell your uncle I'm sorry for all the trouble I caused?"

Lupe told him.

"It's not any trouble," Lupe translated his answer. "He just said it might take a while for you to get used to things out here."

"Well, we don't have monsters in Queens," Ju-Won muttered.

When Mi-Sun opened her eyes the next morning, the first thing she thought about was the strange shape she had seen. It wasn't a dream, or a hallucination—she was sure of it. But what was it? she wondered.

She went to the window. Outside was the backyard, and further behind, the orchard. Nothing looked out of place or strange in the cheerful morning light.

After getting dressed, she went outside.

"Aren't you going to have breakfast?" Lupe called to her from the door.

"I will in a second."

Lupe came out with her. "Did you lose something?"

Mi-Sun felt very silly. She was glad Lupe was such a good friend and probably wouldn't laugh at her.

"I'm looking for footprints or something," she admitted. "Of that thing I saw last night."

"I'll help you look," said Lupe. Mi-Sun wanted to give her friend a hug.

"I think I saw it over there, by that big tree in the yard," Mi-Sun said. The two girls walked over there.

"Here are some tracks," said Lupe. "But I think they're Tuki's. In fact, I definitely think they're Tuki's."

"Hey, but what about these?" said Mi-Sun, pointing. In the ground were some roundish shapes. They were shaped almost like a human foot, but much rounder, like a foot that oozed out of its footprint.

"Do you think those are tracks?" said Lupe. "Do they go anywhere?"

"They do," said Mi-Sun, her heart starting to speed up a little. "See, they alternate and go in a pretty straight line from here to that place, where they get lost in the dry mud."

"I've never seen tracks like that," said Lupe.

"And it's of a two-legged thing," said Mi-Sun. "See how with Tuki's tracks you can see all four paws?"

"These are strange," said Lupe. "I'm not sure if they're tracks, though. Should we ask Tío what he thinks?"

"Oh no," said Mi-Sun quickly. "What if it isn't anything? He thinks Ju-Won and I are paranoid already."

"No he doesn't," Lupe said. "He likes you guys—he said you are model guests, you get along fine while he works all day. But if you don't want to ask him, that's okay, too."

"Let's wait and see," said Mi-Sun. She would be curious to see if she was coming down with Ju-Won-disease after all.

Out of Nowhere

On Saturday, Lupe woke up Mi-Sun and Ju-Won extra early.

"Tío's going to take us on a ride into the hills," she told them. "It'll be great—we'll be able to see the whole town of Tierralinda once we get to the top."

María was already in the house. They didn't intend to spy on her, but they all hung back, watching her, before entering the kitchen. A few times, she bowed her head and seemed to laugh at a private joke. But her laugh didn't sound funny at all. If anything, it sounded sinister.

"Doesn't she ever go home?" Lupe whispered to Mi-Sun. "And doesn't she have any other color to wear besides black?"

59

"I'm hungry," Ju-Won whispered back.

They took deep breaths, then stepped into the kitchen.

"*Buenos días,*" they chorused.

"Top o' the morning," said Ju-Won.

Maria quickly set her stone face back on and started to bustle around the kitchen. She had made delicious huevos rancheros again, but she didn't put out any salsa.

Mi-Sun loved the salsa, but she didn't want to be impolite. Maybe María didn't have any more.

"Uh, Lupe?" she said finally. "Do you think there's more salsa?"

"Sure," said Lupe, and she turned to María. "*¿Hay más salsa?*"

Maria muttered something before setting a small bowl in front of them. Ju-Won poached a spoonful before anyone else even touched it.

"You like salsa?" said Lupe. "I like ketchup better."

"I love this salsa," Mi-Sun said. "It could be a teensy bit hotter, but it's very good. How do you say 'delicious' in Spanish?"

"*Muy rica,*" Lupe said, lazily rolling her r's.

"*María, es muy rica,*" said Mi-Sun, who couldn't roll her r's as well as Lupe. But Maria didn't pay any attention. She just kept on cleaning the kitchen as if she were alone. Why was Maria so crabby and strange? Mi-Sun wondered.

On the way out, Lupe grabbed a few oranges from a huge bowl of fruit sitting on the counter, making sure María's back was turned. "María makes me feel like I'm stealing from my own house," she muttered as they went outside. "I miss Consuela."

Tío Héctor was outside putting wooden saddles on the burros. He said something to Lupe in Spanish.

"Tío said he's sorry we couldn't do this earlier—he's been so busy on the ranch," Lupe translated.

"Ay," Mi-Sun said. "Tell him not to worry."

The saddles had huge wooden horns, bigger than Mi-Sun's whole hand.

"I like this," said Ju-Won. "Something major to hold on to."

"I've never ridden a burro," Mi-Sun remarked to Lupe. "Or a horse, either, for that matter."

"Burros are better because they're steadier," Lupe said. "Horses are faster, but they're more likely to trip and fall."

"Oh great," said Ju-Won. "You mean we might go splat and break all our bones? Can an ambulance get up that hill?"

"Agi, you have a knack for finding a cloud in every silver lining," huffed Mi-Sun. Ju-Won was the only person she knew who could take the fun out of a trail ride.

Tío Héctor made them all wear long pants and hats to keep out the sun.

"He said there are going be lots of sticks and *huachapuri*," said Lupe.

"Huachapuri?" said Mi-Sun.

"Those things," said Lupe, pointing to her donkey's flanks. Mi-Sun saw burrs, the same kind that had tormented Tuki so badly, stuck there like Velcro.

"Hey, maybe that's why they call them burr-os," chimed Ju-Won.

They climbed onto their burros. To Mi-Sun, it felt like riding a large shaggy dog; she kept thinking her feet were going to scrape the ground. But she liked her burro. It had pretty eyes with long lashes and dainty ears that flicked back and forth.

As el sol rose in the sky, they climbed the hills. Mi-Sun thought how different this was from Queens! There was so much sky and land. No rumbling of the Number 7 subway train, no planes taking off and landing at JFK and La Guardia airports, no wheeze of the bus and honking cars. Instead there were plenty of trees, squat plants with sharp-looking leaves, cacti, huge ferns and grasses that looked like something out of *The Land of the Lost,* and blue sky that seemed to go on forever.

"Wow, it's hot," said Ju-Won. "I could really use a paleta."

Of course, there were no paletas to be had. But when they got to the top, they shared some fruit.

There was a nice breeze on the hill and a wonderful view of Tierralinda. They could see how the road into town gently curved behind them. The farms below looked like toys.

The burros idly chewed at plants or dozed standing up. Tío Héctor and Ju-Won put their hats over their faces and napped. Lupe climbed onto a ledge and started to take some pictures.

Mi-Sun wanted to see more of the hill. She headed to the other side, where she found herself in the middle of a stand of trees and had to walk quite a ways until she came to a clearing. When she could see the sky again, she noticed that it had turned a weird turquoise blue, and the birds had stopped singing.

She should probably start heading back. Maybe Tío Héctor had woken up by now and was wondering where she'd gone. She'd only meant to wander off a bit, but she suspected she had gone a lot farther than she'd thought.

She turned around and pushed through the plants again. A cold breeze came out of nowhere, and she was startled to hear a crack of thunder. The sky turned dark. How did that happen? It had been totally clear two minutes ago.

She walked faster. She wasn't exactly sure of the way she'd come, but she figured all she had to do was walk, and she'd get back to the other side.

Suddenly, ahead of her, the grasses started rustling, and she heard the sound of breaking twigs. Something big was moving in front of her—and it was coming her way!

Black as the Night

The grasses parted. Mi-Sun half expected a big, fanged chupacabra to walk out, but it was only the abuelo. He was making his way down the path with a cane, and he was huffing slightly.

"Hola," he said.

"Hola," she replied.

"*¿Cómo estás?*" he said.

"Bien," she was going to answer, but then she blurted: "I'm lost! Everyone else is on the other side of the hill somewhere."

There was a flash of lightning, and Mi-Sun realized that the sky had become black as night. Another crack of thunder!—this time so close it sounded like the sky was about to rip apart like an old sack. Abuelo's brows furrowed as he looked up to the sky.

"*Vente,*" he said, pointing to a small overhang on the hill. "Come."

"I need to find the others," Mi-Sun said.

Just then, a hole tore in the clouds and heavy rain came tumbling down.

Mi-Sun felt a firm hand grip her elbow. Abuelo was leading her to the overhang. Even though he limped, his path was sure and straight, and they found a bit of shelter next to the hill. More lightning divided the sky, and the thunder sounded louder than cannons. Mi-Sun wanted to cover her ears, but she held on to the tree for dear life. She could hear the gurgle of water as it rushed down the sides of the hill, sounding as if it might wash them away.

Then, almost as quickly as the storm had started, it ended. The sun came out as hot as before, the water dripped softly off the trees. The birds resumed their songs, mid-note.

"Whew!" said Mi-Sun. "What was that all about?"

Abuelo looked at her and grinned. "Fast rain," he said.

"I need to find them," she said, pointing in the direction where she thought Tío, Lupe, and Ju-Won were.

Abuelo nodded and started off in that direction, too, following her. The ground was now spongy, and it smelled warm, like bread baking.

"Ay!" cried Tío Héctor when he saw Mi-Sun. He started speaking in rapid Spanish. They were all slightly damp, too, but had taken cover under a tarp Tío Héctor had brought with him.

"Sorry, Tío Héctor," Mi-Sun said. "I wandered off a little too far. Luckily, I ran into Abuelo and he showed me where to hide from the rain."

Lupe translated this for her uncle.

Tío Héctor looked over at the abuelo. *"Muchas gracias, Abuelo Pablo,"* he said.

"De nada," said Abuelo.

"I'm Mi-Sun, by the way," said Mi-Sun. Abuelo smiled.

"Cuauhtemoc Pablo Alvarez de Ortiz," he said, bowing with a flourish. Then he waved to all of them and started down the hill. Even though he limped, his legs looked very strong.

Tío Héctor watched him go, and said something to Lupe in Spanish.

"Tío says Abuelo Pablo used to be the fastest runner in the village—he used to win all the prizes when Tío was a little kid," Lupe translated. "He broke his leg when a horse fell on him, but he still walks everywhere."

Mi-Sun felt bad for Abuelo. She wondered if he walked the hills often. If she lived in Tierralinda, she would come up here all the time and stare out at the tiny town below. Maybe she'd bring her sketchbook.

When they were back at the Rancho de Cabras, Tío Héctor went out into the field to do some work before lunch.

"I want more fruit," said Ju-Won, going into the kitchen. "Hey!" he said suddenly, screeching to a stop in front of the counter. "What's up with this?"

"What?" said Mi-Sun, following.

"There's no fruit left in the bowl," he said, pointing

to the bowl of fruit, which was now completely empty—no oranges, no mangoes, no limes, no coconuts.

"And hey," Ju-Won leaned over the sink. "Look in the sink!"

"What?" said Lupe and Mi-Sun.

Individual pieces of fruit were piled in the sink, looking as if the insides had been sucked out, leaving just the carcasses behind.

Ju-Won picked up a lime. It looked a like collapsed rubber ball.

"It's like someone—or something—sucked this thing dry," he said slowly.

Lupe held a coconut in her hand. She bounced it gently up and down, as if weighing it.

"Strange," she said, handing it to Mi-Sun. It felt rough and hairy, like it was covered in burlap.

"Dry," said Lupe. "See how light it is? No milk." The two girls and Ju-Won craned their heads over the fruit.

"Look!" Ju-Won cried suddenly. "Look at this!" He jabbed at the coconut with his finger.

At the top of the coconut were two neat little holes.

"Chupacobra!" he yelled.

"Chupacabra," Mi-Sun automatically corrected. "And that means *goat* sucker. Whatever this thing is, it's sucking fruit."

"Chupacoco, then," said Ju-Won. *"¿Está bien, hermana?"*

"Hey, your Spanish is getting pretty good," Mi-Sun couldn't help remarking.

"Ay," said Lupe. "This is so strange. Do you think what the abuelo said about the chupacabras is real?"

"Hey, yeah," said Ju-Won. "And it's just practicing on fruit first, before it tries to chupa Ju-Won!" He turned as pale as coconut meat.

"Ju-Won, you're letting your imagination run away with you again," said Mi-Sun. But she couldn't help thinking about the strange things that had happened. What about last night, with that huge shadowy thing she saw creeping out in the yard—and the weird blurry tracks?

"Ay! *¡Niños!*" María suddenly stormed into the kitchen like a big black cloud. The two wings of her thick eyebrows went up and down like birds taking off. "*¡Fuera! ¡Váyanse! ¡Ahora!*" she said, practically swatting them away.

Mi-Sun, Lupe, and Ju-Won scattered and ran into the yard.

"Wow, that's the most I ever heard her say the whole time we've been here," Ju-Won remarked. "What's her problem? We didn't mess anything up."

"She must be one of those people who don't like kids," Lupe suggested. "Tío says she never had children."

"It's probably because she'd eat them," said Ju-Won.

"Ju-Won," Mi-Sun said warningly before she began to wonder out loud: "Why would María get so upset about us being in the kitchen?" It was all too strange, María's laughing to herself, her stony silences, now this.

"Even if she was a neat freak or something, there's

no reason to scream at us," said Lupe. "She seemed upset—like she was hiding something."

They looked at each other. Was Maria somehow mixed up with this whole chupacabra thing?

You could almost hear three brains working.

"I'll bet *she's* the chupacabra!" exclaimed Ju-Won.

Illegal Aliens

The next day, when they went to the panadería, they passed Abuelo, who was sitting in his usual spot in front of the tienda.

Lupe was the first to stop. *"Díganos más sobre los chupacabras, por favor,"* tell us more about the chupacabras, please, Lupe asked him in Spanish.

Abuelo pushed up his straw hat and scratched his head. Then he massaged his neck as if it was sore, and sighed. "Chupacabras all around México."

He said "Mexico" like "Mehico." "In Puerto RRRRico and maybe in el Norte, too!"

"Brr," said Ju-Won, picturing chupacabras in Queens.

"Don't worry," Mi-Sun said to him. "They don't know how to take the subway."

70

"Ha-ha," Ju-Won said darkly.

"Where do you think they come from?" said Lupe.

Abuelo shrugged.

"No sé," he said, and then he pointed to the sky. "Maybe up there. Come from sky."

Mi-Sun pictured the hideous flying monkeys in *The Wizard of Oz.*

"From outer space," said Ju-Won, nodding. "They're space aliens. That makes total sense."

Lupe was looking worried. Ju-Won echoed her thoughts:

"What if María isn't a cook at all, but an alien?" he said. "Maybe chupas can take human form during the day, but what gives her away is that she's like Mr. Spock on *Star Trek* and see, no matter how she tries, she can't do human things like smile. And have you noticed how she never seems to cook the food, how it's just *there* all the time? The aliens probably do research on what humans eat to fool us, but their slip-up is that they don't know that we actually *cook* the food. They probably make it up whole from some kind of alien plasma."

"Oh please, Ju-Won," Mi-Sun said. "That's it! Your horror books are going into the *basura* the minute we get back."

"Let's go to the mercado," said Lupe suddenly. "I need to get something."

Grateful for the change of scenery, Mi-Sun agreed. As they said goodbye to Abuelo, Mi-Sun suddenly wished he'd never brought up the subject of the chupacabras.

The mercado was not far. In fact, in la downtown,

nothing was too far from anything. If they lived in Tierralinda, they would probably never have to take a subway or a bus or a car ever again.

The mercado reminded Mi-Sun of the market in Korea that she went to with O-Ma when she was a little kid, before they came to the U.S. Like the Korean market, the mercado contained many kind of "stores" under one big tent: a fruit stand bursting with mangoes, coconuts, pineapples; another stand with chile peppers braided in long ropes, cilantro, and avocados. One store sold only cheese, another chocolate. There was even a butcher, where the slabs of meat just hung in the air.

At the other end of the tent was the "home" section. They walked past a stall with wallets and shoes, one that sold plastic buckets and other household doodads, one with slingshots, and another selling lassos.

"Hey, here are the slingshots," Mi-Sun pointed out to Ju-Won. "Remember? You said you wanted one."

"Actually, I want to get a rope instead," said Ju-Won, stopping at the lasso stall.

"Really, why?" asked Mi-Sun.

"To catch the chupacabra, dummy," he said, peering at the selection. The man at the stall let him try one. He twirled it around his head like he'd seen cowboys do in movies.

"Yeah, good luck," Mi-Sun said.

"I'll practice," Ju-Won said determinedly. He pulled out some pesos. "Just enough of my allowance left," he declared, handing it to the man, who carefully coiled the rope, tied it with a giant twistee, and handed it him.

At a nearby stall, Lupe stopped and examined some things that looked like blankets. She spoke to the woman and selected a purple one.

"This is a *rebozo*," she explained. "Ladies use them as shawls or to carry babies."

"You can carry agi Ju-Won in it," Mi-Sun offered. She half expected Ju-Won to say something in protest, but he and Lupe gave each other secret looks. Mi-Sun wondered what was going on.

While they were on the way home, they ran into Abuelo on the road.

He said something in Spanish to Lupe, who puckered her mouth.

"He's asking if Tío has any work for him," she told them while Abuelo waited in the distance. "He wants to find a job besides the one he has sweeping at the tienda."

"Maybe Tío Héctor does have work," Mi-Sun said. "With all the goats and animals and things."

"But that's ranch work. Abuelo is kind of old."

"But he's strong," said Mi-Sun. "And brave—he pulled me out of the storm. Besides, you don't want anyone to accuse you of age discrimination, right?"

"Okay, okay," Lupe said. "Abuelo can come with us. He can wait until Tío gets home."

At Rancho de Cabras, Abuelo showed Ju-Won how to use the lasso.

"*Mira*," he said. With a flick of his wrist, he snagged tree stumps, tree branches, and goats. He tried to lasso a chicken, but it was too fast for him.

When Ju-Won threw the rope, it flew all over the

place. He would never catch a cabra—let alone a chupacabra, thought Mi-Sun.

They were still practicing when Tío Héctor came home. Lupe told her uncle about Abuelo's request.

Tío Héctor nodded thoughtfully. He shook hands with Abuelo, who stood tall and said "Gracias." Lupe translated their conversation: he would start work on the ranch tomorrow.

"Gracias, Tío Héctor, gracias!" Mi-Sun said to Tío Héctor, impulsively giving him a hug. Tío Héctor looked a little startled, but then he smiled and said something.

"Tío said there's always plenty to do around the ranch," said Lupe. "And he's always willing to oblige people looking for honest work."

Tío Héctor was wonderful, Mi-Sun decided.

That night, before bed, Lupe and Ju-Won came into Mi-Sun's room. They were wearing pieces of the purple rebozo around their necks like scarves.

Lupe handed her a piece of the rebozo.

"Is it supposed to get cold out tonight?" Mi-Sun asked.

"No, this is to keep the chupacabras away," Ju-Won said. "I don't think it can bite through all this fabric."

Mi-Sun couldn't believe him. Nor could she believe that Lupe was also doing it.

"Lupe, you're in on this?" she said.

"It was Lupe's idea," said Ju-Won. "And I think it's a good one."

Mi-Sun turned her eyes to her friend.

"We-ell," Lupe said a little sheepishly. "You never know."

"Ay," was all Mi-Sun could say. If there was a chupacabra running around out there, a piece of cloth was not going to stop it.

"You don't have to do it," Ju-Won said. "We're just offering it to you because we're nice."

"Good night!" said Mi-Sun.

Mi-Sun went to bed, bone-tired. The moon would be full soon. Its bright light shone like a comforting nightlight into her room.

Later, after she had fallen asleep, she opened her eyes for just a second, and thought she saw a humped shadow pass by her window. But it was silent, as was Tuki. She got up and pulled the piece of rebozo from where she'd left it, on the chair. It was woolly and scratchy, but she put it around her neck, anyway, and fell back asleep.

Eerie Scratching Noises
in Broad Daylight

Mi-Sun was awakened early the next morning by a persistent scratching noise.

SHHhh-SHHhh!

SHHhh-SHHhh!

SHHhh-SHHhh!

What could it be? From her window, she could see nothing. The air was still, almost strangely so, which made the scratching noise seem eerier, louder. And it *wasn't* Tuki.

"Better I find it than it finds me," Mi-Sun decided, as she quickly dressed and slipped on her huaraches. She slipped outside and peeked around the corner of the house.

Abuelo was on the walk, sweeping it with a broom made out of twigs.

SHHhh-SHHhh.

SHHhh-SHHhh.

He looked up and smiled when he saw her. One eye blue, the other brown.

"Buenos días!" he said.

"Buenos días!" she answered. A broom, she thought with relief.

SHHhh-SHHhh.

SHHhh-SHHhh.

Abuelo looked pretty serious about his work, so Mi-Sun smiled at him and went back in the house.

María was standing at the kitchen counter kneading dough. So much for Ju-Won's theory of the food magically appearing, thought Mi-Sun. If he got up earlier, he would see it wasn't so supernatural.

María's arms looked like rolls of soft dough themselves as she energetically folded and punched the mixture.

"Tortillas?" Mi-Sun found herself asking. María looked up. She didn't say anything, but motioned for her to come closer.

Mi-Sun glanced at María's face, hoping she might be able to catch a glimpse of fangs or other evidence.

Stop it! she chastised herself. She was starting to think like Ju-Won, she realized—look how she was rattled by Abuelo Pablo's sweeping.

María motioned for her to wash her hands.

"Mira," she said, and Mi-Sun watched as she added water to the dough and a pinch of some white chalky stuff that must have been the lime Lupe had bought. Then she mixed the whole thing expertly with her hands until it formed a ball.

Without missing a beat, she put some flour from a bag that said MASA in another bowl and indicated that Mi-Sun should add water. Then María nodded and watched Mi-Sun knead the dough, stopping her once to add a pinch of lime.

But Mi-Sun's dough didn't form a ball; instead it stuck uncomfortably to her hands like glue. The more she kneaded it, the more entrapped her fingers became. At this rate, she would probably have to wear the bowl for the rest of the summer.

María grunted and added more flour. Mi-Sun kept kneading, and bit by bit, it peeled off her fingers.

María broke off a bit of dough and rolled it into a ball. She patted it between her palms until it became a perfect circle. Then she dropped it onto the hot skillet, which made a satisfied sighing sound.

Mi-Sun tried for circles, but her dough ended up in ovals, ellipses, and shapes that had no name. Her tortillas were thicker and tougher than María's, and not as flat, more like pancakes than the soft tortillas they used as edible wrappers for their food. Still, María stacked the cooked tortillas together, the little arms and legs and tails of Mi-Sun's thick tortillas sticking out like sassy tongues. María wrapped them in a cloth to keep them warm.

At breakfast, Mi-Sun proudly announced that she'd helped María make the tortillas.

"Not too pukey," offered Ju-Won by way of a compliment. "This one looks like an amoeba before it replicates."

"These are great," said Lupe.

María bustled about the kitchen, putting things

away. She might not be the friendliest of people, but she wasn't so bad, thought Mi-Sun. How could they have thought she might be a chupacabra?

Tuki came clicking into the kitchen and Ju-Won dropped a crescent moon of tortilla into her mouth, which was open like a mailbox.

"Don't feed the dog at the table," Mi-Sun scolded. Then she added, "Besides, I thought you were scared of Tuki—didn't you see her teeth?"

Ju-Won paused for a second. "I'm not scared of her anymore," he said. "In fact, I think she sleeps with me at night to protect me from the chupacabras."

"¿Qué?" said Maria, as she turned from the sink.

Ju-Won clamped his mouth shut, and he and Lupe looked fearfully at each other.

Come on, Mi-Sun thought. They couldn't be serious.

After chores, the three went outside. Ju-Won practiced swinging his rope while Lupe and Mi-Sun fed one of the goats from a baby bottle. Its mother had been the goat that was killed. With its sweet eyes and big, droopy ears, the baby goat was darling even with milk dribbling down its chin. The older goats were cute, too; their curvy horns and beards made them look like little preachers.

The girls sat listening to the goats contentedly maaing. Occasionally, they caught glimpses of Abuelo slowly pushing a wheelbarrow, carrying a shovel, or hauling wood. And every so often they would hear Ju-Won say "Heh!"—which meant he had successfully roped the tree stump. Tuki sat in the shade and watched all the proceedings with interest.

"Look," Ju-Won said to them. "I can almost catch the doorknob on the barn."

He threw the lasso, which looped over the doorknob, but then fell.

"Make the loop smaller," Lupe suggested. "You only need a big loop for big targets."

Ju-Won obligingly made the loop smaller. In two tries, he caught the knob. He went over to the door to free the loop.

"Ick," he said. "There's a huge spider right by the knob."

"Just knock it away," said Mi-Sun.

Ju-Won stared at the spider. Twice he made a small move toward it. Twice he stopped.

"Yuuggghhh," he said. "That sucker is *huge,* like those man-eating spiders in *Spiders from Mars Ate My Brain.*"

"Don't be such an agi," said Mi-Sun.

"Okay, you do it, Nuna," said Ju-Won. "Remove the big hairy spider."

Mi-Sun went toward the spider. When she got closer, she saw how big it was. It wasn't just that it had long legs like the *macacos,* daddy longlegs, but this spider's *body* was big as well. It was the largest, blackest spider she had seen that wasn't in a museum or a horror movie.

She picked up a stick to brush it away, but lost her nerve, wondering if it might suddenly fly up and attack her or something.

"Ugh, I can't do it, either," she admitted.

"Hey, Abuelo!" Ju-Won yelled. Abuelo put down his

shovel. "I can't get my rope off the door *porque hay una araña grande!*"

Abuelo walked over to the rope and then saw the araña, the spider.

"Ay!" he yelled, but it came out as a whisper. *"Muy peligrosa!"*

Viuda Negra

Abuelo picked up the shovel. He started whanging away at the spider until it was just a small pile of wet mush.

"Muy peligrosa," he said again.

"Peligrosa," repeated Mi-Sun. Dangerous!

"Una viuda negra," said Abuelo, panting a little. There was sweat shining all over his face.

"Ay," said Lupe, turning white as a sheet. "Abuelo said that thing was a black widow."

"A black widow?" asked both Ju-Won and Mi-Sun.

Mi-Sun had read in science class about how the black widow has a red hourglass shape on her belly and fangs covered in poison. She shivered, remembering how relieved she'd been to learn they were warm-weather creatures and couldn't survive in New York. But she *was* in sunny Mexico. What if that thing had bitten Ju-Won or her? Peligrosa!

Ju-Won was still too scared to undo his lasso from the barn door, so Abuelo took it off for him. He said *"Cuidado"* to Lupe, which she translated as "Be careful." Now they had one more entry on their growing list of things to watch out for: black widows, scorpions, and of course, chupacabras.

"Gracias, Abuelo," said Mi-Sun. "Muchas gracias."

"De nada." Abuelo gave them a little wave, flicking his wrist the same way he did when he threw the rope. He wiped his shovel in the sand and walked off.

"See, he's not too old," Mi-Sun said to Lupe. Lupe, still white, nodded in agreement.

When Tío Héctor found out what Abuelo had done, he offered him a crate of beer. Abuelo blushed and said no, it was nothing, and besides, he didn't drink.

Then Tío Héctor offered him a goat. Abuelo looked thoughtful. He might like a goat, he said finally. He lived by himself in a shack on the edge of town, and he had a little yard where he could raise a goat.

"Escoja la cabra que usted quiera," said Tío Héctor, telling Abuelo to pick any goat. *"Una que le da mucha carne"*—one that will give you lots of meat.

Abuelo chose the baby goat, the one without a mother. That goat would be too much trouble, Tío Héctor told him; without its mother's milk it would probably die. But Abuelo didn't budge. He thanked

Tío Héctor profusely, then left, leading the little goat by a string.

"Maaaaaa!" said the goat, its tail wagging back and forth rapidly like a windshield wiper as it followed Abuelo home.

Night Fright

In the middle of the night, Mi-Sun sat straight up. Tuki was barking. Soon, she heard howls and yips from other dogs in the area, like a canine chorus.

She ran to her window. There was something big out in the yard!

She ran to Tío Héctor's room.

"Tío Héctor! Wake up!" she said, pounding on the door. In seconds, Tío Héctor opened the door.

"In the yard!" said Mi-Sun. "There's something in the yard!"

Tuki pawed at the door, growling. When they opened it, she ran out like a shot and disappeared into the night.

They heard fierce growls, then a sharp YIPE!

Mi-Sun ran in the direction

85

of the sounds even though she was barefoot. Where was Tuki?

Almost as fast as she had gone, Tuki was back. The fur on her back was standing up, coming to a sharp point. She was limping, and there was blood on her paw.

"Oh, Tuki," Mi-Sun said, examining her paw. It looked like it had been bitten.

Lupe appeared behind her. "Do you think it was a chupacabra?" she whispered to Mi-Sun.

"It was something big," Mi-Sun said.

There was a rustling noise, and both girls turned to see María coming out from behind the house. What the heck was she doing there? wondered Mi-Sun. They were all in their pajamas, but Maria was fully dressed in her usual black.

Lupe gulped. *"¿María, por qué no está en su casa?"* she asked. *"Ya hace muy tarde."*

Mi-Sun was thinking the same thing: why wasn't Maria at her home at this late hour?

"Tengo algo que hacer," said María—I have things to do.

"¿Como qué?" Like what? Lupe said, a little suspiciously.

"Nada importante," said María evasively. Mi-Sun burned with curiosity. What was up?

The next day, Mi-Sun and Lupe went out into the yard to investigate. The weird, blurry tracks had re-appeared in the yard.

"Ay," said Lupe. "So strange, these things!"

"What could it possibly be?" wondered Mi-Sun with

a shudder. The tracks, before they disappeared, were pointing right toward the house!

"Not good, whatever it is," said Lupe. "If this keeps happening, I think we should tell Tío."

"*¿Qué?*" said Tío. He came out from the goat pen carrying a water bucket.

Mi-Sun and Lupe looked at each other. Mi-Sun was just about to ask Tío Héctor about the tracks when Lupe broke in.

Why doesn't María ever seem to go home? she complained to Tío Héctor in Spanish.

"*Esta es su hogar. Vive en la casita en la huerta.*"

"She lives here? In a house out in the orchard?" said Lupe. "That's so strange."

"*¿No tiene una familia?*" She doesn't have a family? Mi-Sun asked, suddenly proud of how much Spanish she had learned.

Tío shook his head. "*Es una viuda.*"

A viuda? Where had she heard that word? Mi-Sun wondered.

"She's a widow," said Lupe.

"Oh," said Mi-Sun. "She's a viuda negra—remember, black widow?"

"That's for sure," muttered Lupe.

Tío walked back into the field, just as Mi-Sun realized she had forgotten to ask him about the tracks.

"Ay," said Tío Héctor the next day. "*Algo está tratando de lastimar a las cabras.*"

"Something's still trying to get at the goats," said Lupe.

"Are they all right?" asked Mi-Sun worriedly. *"¿Está bien?"*

"Sí, pero nervosas," he said. *"Que bueno que tú nos despertiste."*

"He said they're fine, but nervous—it was good you woke us up," said Lupe. She rubbed her neck. It was a little red and creased where the wool rebozo had chafed it.

Mi-Sun decided to write a letter to her parents. She had already had letters from both her mother and father. She had meant to write to them sooner, but something would happen and she would forget.

Today for sure, she decided.

"I'm writing to my folks, finally," she informed Lupe.

"Are you going to tell them about the chupacabras?" asked Lupe.

Mi-Sun sighed. "I should say *something,* don't you think?" If anything happened, people in el norte needed to know.

Dear O-Ma and Ah-Pa,

She wrote the first part in Korean, to show she hadn't forgotten it while she was down here.

Sorry it took me so long to write. Being in Mexico is great. The ranch is great: it has chickens and goats running around all over it. Ju-Won (we call him "Juan" down here— ha-ha) is learning how to use a lasso.

There was so much to tell: about Tuki, the rancho, paletas. She started to tell them about Abuelo, how he saved her from the thunderstorm, and how he saved Ju-Won from the black widow. But then she decided they would probably think Mexico was very dangerous. Anyway, she had written almost three pages and her fingers had fallen asleep from pressing so hard on the pen. She quickly ended the letter:

By the way, the old grandpa ("abuelo") on the rancho keeps telling us stories about these things called chupacabras, which means "goat sucker." No one knows for sure if they really exist—sort of the way some people in America think there are aliens from outer space—but we are keeping a watch over the goats just to be sure.

She was going to add *Some people (including Lupe and Ju-Won) think Maria, the cook, might possibly be a chupacabra.* But then she didn't. That would be like accusing someone of stealing without evidence.

I miss you, and hope everything's going well at home and at the store. Your loving daughter, Mi-Sun.

She wrote the last part in Korean and looked at it with satisfaction.

"Cool," said Lupe. She was always impressed with how Korean looked, the different letters interlocking like pictures. Spanish, although it sounded different, used basically the same alphabet as English, with accent marks.

The two girls went downtown to the post office. Lupe taught her the word for stamps, *timbres,* and they mailed the letter. Of course, they stopped for paletas. Some people were setting up a small stage in the middle of the zócalo.

"Tonight is a fiesta night," said Lupe. "They'll have a band and we can dance."

"That sounds like fun," said Mi-Sun, licking her paleta. She had decided to be daring and try a *tuna* one. It was deep purple with black seeds and tasted like intense watermelon. It was deliciosa.

They went back to the house. Tuki wagged her tail when she saw them, and Ju-Won finally had woken up. Mi-Sun couldn't wait to tell him about the excitement he'd slept through last night.

"Look at this," said Ju-Won, standing by the sink. He held another coconut. "I just found this lying here. It's empty—and here are those same two holes!"

Mi-Sun and Lupe both gulped.

Fiesta

"I wouldn't mind going home a little early," Mi-Sun was thinking out loud to Ju-Won. "I miss Ah-Pa and O-Ma."

Ju-Won was quiet. He turned his newest book, *My Incredible Intergalactic Adventure,* over onto his chest like a tent. He stared at her.

"Okay," she admitted. "My nerves are totally on edge." Just this afternoon, she had seen a friendly little daddy longlegs on her wall—and almost had a heart attack. And daddy longlegs didn't even have teeth! She had screamed and Abuelo Pablo had come running, and then she didn't know how to explain in Spanish that she had made a mistake. She had been so embarrassed.

"Oh come on, Nuna," said

91

Ju-Won. "We *have* to solve this mystery. I don't want to see Tuki getting hurt again."

Was this Agi talking? "*You* don't miss being home?" she asked.

"Of course I do," he said. "I miss O-Ma and Ah-Pa—but if we were home, you and me would be going to summer school all day."

"You and I would be going to summer school," she corrected.

"Yeah, like I said. Anyway, with us here, there are more ears and eyes to look out for the chupacabra. I think Tío Héctor sleeps almost as soundly as I do!"

"You do have a point," Mi-Sun admitted. Who knew how many goats would have been hurt if she hadn't woken Tío Héctor up the other night? She decided to give Mexico another chance.

Lupe loaned Mi-Sun a Mexican sundress for the fiesta. Mi-Sun liked how cool, yet dressed up, it made her look, and it went perfectly with her huaraches. Ju-Won was wearing a straw cowboy hat, the kind Abuelo and Tío Héctor wore, jeans, and his huaraches. From the way he strutted around, you could tell he was pretty pleased.

As el sol set, they all made their way to the zócalo. Mi-Sun could hear music and laughing, and she could smell crisp *elotes*, ears of corn, cooking in their husks on a flame. She was excited again about being in Mexico.

It seemed like everyone in town was there, dressed to the nines. The band played catchy guitar music that Lupe told Mi-Sun was called *ranchera*. A couple of boys asked Lupe to dance, but she said no, that she'd wait until there was someone to dance with her friend, too.

The two girls ate elotes, which were on sticks, like paletas. They had them with butter, lime, and hot chile powder, although Lupe told the man to go easy on the chile.

"You are a wimp!" Mi-Sun teased.

"I don't have an asbestos mouth, like you," Lupe retorted.

When they were done with their elotes, two brothers asked them to dance. Lupe nodded. Mi-Sun told her she had no idea what to do.

"Easy—it's just one-two, one-two," Lupe said, lightly tapping out a beat. When she and the boy started dancing, they took off like one graceful unit, as if they were attached to the music.

The other brother grinned as Mi-Sun tried to get the hang of the beat. She hopped from one foot to the other like a chicken on hot sand. They were staying in place while everyone else was flowing like water around them.

"*Sígame,*" he said with a smile. She had no idea what he was saying, but she felt his hand on her waist push a little, and his other hand took hers and he guided her through the crowd. She stopped concentrating on the one-two, one-two, and they started to move.

"Hey, that was fun!" she said to him when the song ended. "Muchas gracias!"

"*¿No hablas español?*" said the boy. He had a crescent of gold in a tooth, which seemed to smile with him.

Mi-Sun shook her head, then ran off to find Lupe.

It was amazing how everyone in Tierralinda was at the fiesta. She couldn't imagine getting everyone in their Queens neighborhood together. Even little babies were out, some sleeping peacefully inside their mothers' rebozos, others staring wide-eyed at all the action.

Mi-Sun, Ju-Won, and Lupe watched the people dance. Tío Héctor danced by with some woman and waved. A guy went around selling tacos made out of *machaca*. Lupe said this meant burro meat, but Mi-Sun didn't want to believe her.

"Did you have fun dancing?" Lupe asked Mi-Sun.

"It was pretty fun, actually," said Mi-Sun. "Once I got the hang of it. But every time I started concentrating on what my feet were doing, I started stepping on that guy's toes. How was the other brother?"

"They're cousins," said Lupe. "I was dancing with Vicente, the older one—wasn't he cute? He was a great dancer, too. Actually, your guy, Emilio, had a nice smile."

Ju-Won made a face. "Don't you have anything better to talk about?" he huffed. "I'm going to go find myself a paleta."

"But he was cute, don't you think?" said Lupe, after Ju-Won had left.

"I guess so," said Mi-Sun. "I didn't really see him."

"Ay," said Lupe, but it came out soft, more like an exhalation.

*   *   *

For once, there were absolutely no cars in the zócalo. But Mi-Sun saw something moving, coming into
sight on the street. Even when it was still far away,
she could see it was Abuelo, pedaling a rickety bike.
They heard a roar of friendly laughter as he passed,
and some people yelled *"Ay! Cuidado! ¡Viejo loco!"*
Watch out—crazy old man!

When he came closer, the girls saw what the com-
motion was about.

In the basket in the back, a pink bow on its head,
was the baby goat, just its head and little hooves
sticking out.

Someone in the crowd yelled something, and everyone laughed.

"Ay." Lupe laughed. "That guy just said 'I'm gonna
have your little goat for supper!' No way, though, that
goat is the abuelo's little niña."

Abuelo made a couple of triumphant circles in the
zócalo. He waved when he saw Lupe and Mi-Sun, and
they waved back.

"Maaaaa!" said the little goat. The girls laughed so
hard they thought their sides would split.

Setting the Trap

Ju-Won was now practicing roping people. He made either Lupe or Mi-Sun stand still for ages as he practiced throwing the loop over them. Sometimes he practiced on Tuki, who took her duty very seriously and stood stock-still even when the rope bonked her in the snout.

"Agi, I'm hot," Mi-Sun complained.

"I have to practice," he insisted. "How else am I going to catch the chupacabra?"

"You *want* to catch the chupacabra?"

"Look, if we don't catch him first, who knows what'll happen? Maybe he'll have babies."

"Not if it's a *he,*" said Mi-Sun.

"With chupacabras, you never know—it could clone itself like the alien creature in *The Many-Headed Monster from Planet Cerberus,*" he replied, tossing the loop yet again. It settled with some dust, halfway on Mi-Sun's shoulders. She coughed.

For the last week, though, the goats had been fine. Abuelo and Tío Héctor checked the fences every other day to make sure there were no holes.

No more sucked-dry coconuts showed up, either. No scorpions, no black widows—unless you counted María. Life was as calm as could be.

"I'm going to get up early tomorrow," Ju-Won announced.

"Oh, before noon?" his sister teased him.

IIe glared back at her. "Nuna, I'll need your help as backup. I'm going to try to catch the chupacabra in the kitchen. Don't you notice how the punctured coconuts usually appear in the morning?"

"Agi," said Mi-Sun. "We aren't living in a *Scream Street* book."

"Just get up, okay?"

Ju-Won put his alarm clock, which he hadn't used all summer, under his pillow so it wouldn't wake anyone else.

That night, Mi-Sun dreamed she and Lupe were on the subway. Then it turned into an airplane that was taking them into New York City. Sitting next to them was a man wearing dark glasses. When he took them off, she saw he was green and scaly like Swamp Thing, and that he was sucking on a coconut.

"The chupacabra!" she screamed and started pulling Lupe out of her seat. But they were going to land,

and the stewardess told them they had to keep their seatbelts on. Mi-Sun clawed at hers anyway, but it was stuck. The chupacabra was biting Lupe on the neck and drinking her blood through a straw.

Mi-Sun yelled again. Suddenly, she woke up and realized there was a hand clamped around her mouth. She was about to bite it when she heard Ju-Won's voice.

"Shhhh! You're going to ruin the whole plan. You gotta stick with me like a huachapuri."

She peeled his hand off her mouth. "I was dreaming Lupe was being eaten by a chupacabra," she explained.

The two of them crept down and hid behind the huge potted palm in the kitchen. The gray light of day was just beginning to make its way into the misty air. A rooster crowed, but all the other animals and people were asleep.

Mi-Sun had never been up so early in her life. Even the air seemed different at this hour. Everything was perfectly still, like the night was breathlessly waiting for the morning to come. Her mind began to wander— what might she have for breakfast?

Then she heard a noise, a heavy footstep that was muffled, as if they were hearing it from inside a bag. She sat bolt upright, and Ju-Won clutched his lasso.

A dark figure lurched into the kitchen. Mi-Sun held her breath. The figure crept over to the bowl of fruit on the counter and started to rummage through it.

Ju-Won sent the rope sailing and they heard a thump as the thing stumbled. Ju-Won pulled the rope tight and started to yell, "The chupacabra! I caught the chupacabra! Help! *¡Ayúdeme! ¡Auxilio!*"

There was a clattering noise and fast footsteps. Mi-Sun ran to turn on the light. Somehow, when it all cleared, they saw María, holding a coconut, trapped inside the lasso.

"Ay!" screamed María, holding up the coconut, as if she were going to throw it.

"Aha!" said Ju-Won. "*You're* the chupacabra."

"¿Chupacabra?" said Maria with puzzlement.

She untangled herself from the rope, recoiled it, and gave it back to Ju-Won.

By this time, Lupe and Tío Héctor had made it to the kitchen.

"See, I caught the chupacabra!" said Ju-Won.

"¿Chupacabra?" said Tío Héctor with a puzzled look on his face. "*¿Dónde?*"

"The thing that's been after the goats, there it is," said Lupe, pointing at María. "*El monstruo que está tratando de lastimar las cabras.*"

"*Chupacabra no hay,*" said Maria, folding her arms.

"María just said she's not a chupacabra," said Lupe.

"*La señora no es un chupacabra,*" said Tío Héctor.

"Uncle also said she's not a chupacabra," said Lupe.

"So ask her what she was doing with the fruit!" said Ju-Won.

"*Entonces, María, ¿qué iba a hacer con la fruta?*"

"Ay, ay, ay," said Maria, putting her hand to her head. She looked like she was going to faint, or she had a huge headache. Mi-Sun shoved a chair near her in case she needed to sit down. She noticed that

María had wrapped her feet in several layers of plastic bags. Was she trying to keep her shoes clean?

"Las frutas," Lupe reminded her.

María sighed. She said something wearily in Spanish.

"Okay," Lupe said. "She said, 'It's hard to keep a secret from you kids—no matter if I stay up late or get up early—you're so nosy!' "

"Her secret's out now!" said Ju-Won. "She's the chupacabra."

Maria held up the coconut and a nail.

"Intento hacer unas paletas de coco y limón," she said. *"Pero necesito mucho jugo. Hago unos agujeros en los cocos, para sacar el jugo y mezclarlo con la fruta. Es aun más difícil sacar el jugo de los limones porque son tan pequeños."*

"Ay," said Lupe, slapping her own head.

"What?" said Ju-Won and Mi-Sun at the same time.

Maria opened the freezer and pulled out a plastic mold, about half-filled, with rough sticks poking out of it.

"Paletas," Lupe explained. "She said it takes a lot of juice to make them and that's why she made the holes in the coconuts with the nail, to drain the juice and mix it with the meat. See, she pokes out the eyes at the top of the coconut; that's why the holes were always in the same place. She says the limes were even worse to get the juice out of because they're so small. That explains all the squished fruit in the sink."

Boy, did they feel stupid!

"But why?" said Mi-Sun. "Why did she go to so much trouble to sneak around to make the paletas?"

Lupe translated: "She said she saw how much we liked them, so she wanted to surprise us with them. She even said she put plastic bags on her feet so her shoes wouldn't click on the floor and wake us up when she came to the kitchen early in the morning. She said she felt like doing something nice for us because she doesn't have kids."

"Mm, that explains the weird tracks," said Mi-Sun.

"Ay!" said Ju-Won. "This is terrible! I can't believe I thought she was the chupacabra."

Now when they looked more closely, the three could see that Maria looked more sad than sinister. She had lost her husband—that must be why she was wearing black—so what was there to smile about? And she didn't have any children. . . .

"We can be your niños for the summer!" Mi-Sun said suddenly. "*Ju-Won, Lupe, y yo los niños de María para el* summer."

"Did you just say we'll be her kids for the summer?" said Ju-Won. "Hey, cool idea."

"That was very close, Mi-Sun," Lupe said, and then she translated the right words: "*Seramos los hijos de María por el verano.*"

María smiled. This was the first time they'd ever seen her smile. She didn't have fangs.

"*¿Qué es esto de los chupacabras?*" asked Tío Héctor.

"Have you heard of them?" Ju-Won asked breathlessly. "*¿Sabes los chupacabras?*"

"Sí," he said, still looking puzzled. *"Son nada más que un cuento para asustar a los pequeños."*

"He says they're just tales made up to scare little kids," Lupe translated.

"So they don't exist?" Mi-Sun said, relieved.

"I guess not."

"Then what killed the goat?" Ju-Won demanded. Lupe asked her uncle.

"He's not sure, but he thinks it was a dog or a coyote," Lupe said.

"So Tío is *sure* they don't exist?" Ju-Won asked.

Tío laughed, and proceeded to tell them a story in Spanish. María also laughed a few times, and nodded her head.

"Tío said when he was a little kid, his mom and dad used to tell him that chupacabras roamed the hills of Tierralinda," translated Lupe. "They told him if he didn't behave, they would put him outside at night, when the chupas would come down from the hills and get him—and boy, did he behave!"

"But does he think they exist? Maybe his parents were telling him the truth," said Ju-Won. *"Tío, ¿los chupacabras no existen?"*

"He says he's never seen one—and he's lived in Tierralinda all his life," said Lupe. "I guess he probably knows best."

"Nice going," Mi-Sun told her brother. "I'm surprised Tío Héctor didn't ship us back to el norte on the next plane for scaring poor María half out of her wits."

"How was I supposed to know?" Ju-Won said.

"Don't tell me you didn't believe in chupacabras just a teeny tiny bit."

"I was undecided," Mi-Sun said. "In any event, you've got to quit reading all those horror books."

"What books?" said Ju-Won. "I've barely had time to read this whole summer."

Mi-Sun noticed that that night Ju-Won and Lupe didn't bother mummifying their necks in the rebozo cloth—and neither did she.

Tamales and Mangoes

María offered to teach the girls how to make tamales.

"That would be great," said Mi-Sun. "And we could have a tamale dinner tonight—yum!"

"*¿Qué hacen hoy?*" What are you doing today, María asked them.

"*Vamos al centro pava buscar los mangos,*" said Lupe with a giggle.

"Did you just say we're going into town to find some mangoes?" said Mi-Sun. "There's plenty right here in this bowl."

"No, silly," said Lupe. "*Mango* is also a cute guy. I want to go downtown and try to find those two brothers."

"Aha," said Mi-Sun.

Not surprisingly, Ju-Won

104

said he would skip the scouting expedition to stay at the Rancho and read. He had started *My Iditarod* only because he was now fresh out of *Scream Street* books, but to Mi-Sun, it seemed like he actually might like the book: his bookmark was almost halfway through.

Mi-Sun and Lupe walked to town. It was a normal weekday, so people were bustling about, but none of them were the two cousins. In fact, they saw mostly señoras doing their shopping. The two girls ate paletas in the shade and watched.

Mi-Sun got restless first.

"I thought you said if we sit here, we'll see everyone," she teased her friend.

"We probably haven't sat here long enough," Lupe said. Then she got up and sighed. "Ay, my legs are killing me from this hard bench. I don't know what I'm thinking. The mangoes must be working on the ranch or the farm or wherever they live."

"They don't get summer vacation?"

Lupe shook her head.

"Uh-uh," she said. "People work harder here—kids, too. Some of Tío's friends think it's so funny that I stay here and don't work."

"Maybe we should," said Mi-Sun.

"But then what would Abuelo Pablo and María do? That's how they earn a living."

"I guess you could consider this work," Mi-Sun said with a laugh. "You're suffering, at least."

*   *   *

The girls sat until siesta time, when they went back to the ranch and took a nap. When they awoke, María had a cool pitcher of lemonade waiting for them.

"*¿Están listos para hacer tamales?*" she asked.

"María wants to know if we're ready to make the tamales," said Lupe.

"Of course!" said Mi-Sun, jumping up. "Bueno!"

"Okay," María said. "*Vámonos a la cocina.*" The two girls followed her into the kitchen.

Maria cleared off the counter, and then she brought in a sheaf of cornhusks. She showed the girls how to tear off shoelace-sized strips. When they had enough, they moved to the stove, where there was a big bowl of shredded pork waiting. Maria sautéed it with chiles, a pinch of salt, and some spices.

"This is just the way my mom makes *mandu*, Korean dumplings!" Mi-Sun exclaimed. "First, she makes a big batch of the meat filling like this."

María put the meat in a clean bowl and then went to the next step, making a batch of dough, just as she did for the tortillas. But this time, she rolled it into a smaller ball and put it into a metal press, which squished it flat. She carefully peeled off the circle of dough and laid it in the center of an open cornhusk. Then she spooned a dollop of filling and some cheese into the middle.

"This *is* like mandu, putting in the filling," said Lupe, for whom Mrs. Kim's beef-and-tofu mandu was a favorite. "This is just Mexican mandu."

María nodded, as if she understood, and then showed them how to gently work the cornhusk and dough around the filling, folding it and tying it with one of the shoestring husk pieces until it made a neat little package.

"All that work for one measly tamale?"

Ju-Won, with Tuki following close at his heels, had wandered into the kitchen. He pushed his way to the counter, and María moved over to make room for him. Tuki curled up by the door and gave them all a doggie half-smile.

"Ju-Won, say excuse me to María," Mi-Sun scolded him.

"Perdóname," Ju-Won said politely to Maria. Then he turned and stuck his tongue out at Mi-Sun. "I bet you and Lupe were fixing to hog all these tamales for yourselves!"

"Darn, you found us out," said Lupe, shaking her head and grinning. "Well, now that you're here, you gotta work if you want to eat. No work, no *comida,* amigo."

It didn't take too much coaxing to get Ju-Won to join the tamale assembly line. After crumbling and crushing the first couple of tamales, the three of them had it down well enough that they could produce a whole pile, neatly tied into bows by Lupe. Then María took the whole plate and showed them how to steam the tamales.

As they finished, Tío Héctor walked into the house from the field. He spied the pile of just-steamed tamales and made a happy noise.

"Tío just said, 'Yippee, tamales—my favorite meal,' " Lupe translated.

"Me too," said Ju-Won. "I'm ready to become a Mexican. Let's eat!"

This time, when they asked María to join them, she did.

"She says she has to make sure the tamales taste okay," Lupe said.

"*¡Muy rica!*" said Mi-Sun, peeling her second one.

"*Sí, muy rica,*" Maria agreed.

Goat Killer

It was the barking that woke Mi-Sun. Tuki!

She ran to her window. There was another, lower growl mixed in with Tuki's barking.

She ran to Ju-Won's room.

"Ju-Won, wake up!" She shook her brother. "Something's outside with Tuki."

Ju-Won leapt up immediately and ran out the door, automatically grabbing his lasso.

The front door was open. There was definitely something entangled with Tuki in the yard.

Ju-Won squinted, aimed, and then let the rope fly. It grew taut and trembling, like fishing line with a big catch on the end.

"Heave ho!" said Ju-Won, pulling tight. Tuki continued to bark as Mi-Sun and Ju-Won pulled off whatever she was fighting. The thing snarled and snapped and scrabbled with its claws.

When the dust cleared, in the moonlight, they could see the ugly dog with the liver-colored spots. It snarled and bristled under the rope, but Ju-Won and Mi-Sun held on tight.

A few feet away from it was a goat, its stomach ripped open.

Paletas

Tío Héctor had the goat-killer dog taken away. He lavishly praised Ju-Won for his rope-throwing skills. When the rodeo came to Tierralinda, he insisted, Ju-Won certainly would have to join the lasso-throwing contest.

"Wow, it feels good to have the mystery solved for sure," Mi-Sun said. She had written to her parents immediately to tell them not to worry about the chupacabras. All this time it had just been a hungry, sneaky dog making its way through Tío Héctor's fences.

"Paletas para los niños héroes," said María as she popped the icy-cold treats out of the mold.

"Viva María!" said Mi-Sun. "Homemade paletas!"

All of them took a paleta,

111

which turned out to be even more delicious than the ones they bought in the zócalo—Maria had put in nuts and extra chunks of fruit. She called Abuelo into the house so he could try one, too.

"¡Deliciosísimo!" declared Abuelo. He still swore up and down that chupacabras existed—he said he had even read about it in the paper—but he had such a sparkle in his eye that Mi-Sun didn't know what to believe.

"Look, I'm a chupapaleta," said Ju-Won, sucking all the juice out of his.

Everyone laughed.

Adiós

Mi-Sun, Lupe, and Ju-Won were amazed at how quickly the remaining weeks passed. Finally, the day came to leave.

"I can't believe it's time to go," Mi-Sun said as she, Lupe and Ju-Won took one last walk along the Rancho.

"Things are going to be so boring back in Queens," said Ju-Won. Mi-Sun noticed that he seemed to stand a little straighter, to act less whiny. This trip had been good for him, she decided.

"I'm going to miss so many things about this ranch," Mi-Sun declared. She tried to make her mind a camera, taking in every-thing: the goats, the hills, the sky.

She especially noted the

113

unique dry/wet terrain. Part desert with cacti and part lush, leafy trees. It hadn't rained in a few days, and the yard was looking dry again. She took a slow walk around the yard, saying goodbye to all the animals, especially her favorite burro, the long-lashed Chiquita.

"Vámonos al aeropuerto," called Tío Héctor finally.

"Let's go," said Mi-Sun, directing them back into the house. They gathered up their bags, which were now heavier because of all the gifts they were bringing to their parents.

María and Abuelo Pablo looked sad, standing in the driveway. María had packed a sackful of snacks to take on the plane. Mi-Sun hoped she'd be back someday to see them again.

Ju-Won could hardly bring himself to say goodbye to Tuki, who was so sad she drooped all over. She licked Ju-Won's face and wagged her tail bravely. When they climbed into the truck, she put her front paws in, too, but Tío Héctor sternly told her no.

Ju-Won let some tears fall as they bounced down the dirt driveway.

"Ul jee ma," stop crying, Mi-Sun said, but she said it more so she wouldn't start crying herself.

"Ay," said Tío Héctor sadly as he stood at the airport's gate.

"Gracias por todo, gracias por todo"—thanks for everything, said Lupe as the three of them hugged him tightly.

"Un momento," said Tío Héctor, and he disappeared behind a sign that said LA MICHOACANA. He reappeared with three paletas.

"Wow, Tío Héctor, how did you know what I want?" said Ju-Won. Tío Héctor just laughed.

The three of them got on the plane. The plane took off, and Mexico became smaller and smaller as the last of the paletas melted, deliciously, in their mouths.

Glossary

Spanish

abierto—open
abuela—grandmother; affectionately, *abuela*
abuelo—grandfather; affectionately, *abuelito*
adiós—goodbye
aeropuerto—airport
alacrán—scorpion
amigo—friend
anoche—last night
araña—spider
ayúdame—help me
auxilia—help
barda—wall
basura—garbage
bien—fine, okay
buenas tardes—good afternoon

bueno—good

buenos días—good morning

cabras—goats

casa de cambio—"house of change," money-changing office

centro—downtown

cerrado—closed

Cinco de Mayo—a May fifth holiday celebrating the Mexican victory over the French at the Battle of Puebla

claro—clear

coco—coconut

comida—food

¿como estás?—how are you?

cría—baby animal

cuidado—be careful

chupas—lollipops

delicioso—delicious

diablo—devil

dónde—where

elote—ear of corn

encuéntrala—find it

espinas—spines

estúpido—stupid

feo—ugly

fruta—fruit

gracias—thank you

hermana—sister

hojarasca—sugar cookie

hola—hello

hoyo—hole

huachapuri—burr

huarache—sandal
huevos—eggs
huevos rancheros—eggs ranch style
jabalina—wild pig
lárgate—go away
limón—lime
macaco—daddy longlegs
machaca—ground meat
madre—mother; affectionately, *mamá*
más—more
masa—flour
mija / mijo—daughter/son, children, "kids"
monstruo—monster
muñeca—doll
muy—very
nada—nothing
negro—black
no hablas español—you don't speak Spanish
noche—night
norteamericanos—"north Americans," Americans
norte (el)—the north, U.S.A.
oreja—ear
paleta—popsicle
panadería—bakery
pan dulce—sweet bread
papel—paper
peligrosa / peligroso—dangerous
perdón—pardon
perdóname—pardon me
perro—dog
peso—Mexican money
piña—pineapple

por favor—please
por todo—for everything
que le vaya bien—goodbye, farewell
rebozo—shawl
recuerdo—souvenir
rica—delicious
salsa—sauce; combinations of vegetables, chile peppers, and spices
sí—yes
siesta—"hot time of day," rest
sol—sun
tamales—a variety of fillings and cornmeal in a wrapper (cornhusks, banana leaves, etc.)
tamarindo—tamarind fruit
tienda—general store
un momento—one moment
tío—uncle
vámonos—let's go
viuda—widow
zapatería—shoe store
zócalo—town center

Korean

abogee—father; affectionately, *ah-pa*
anyonghaseo—hello, how are you?
agi (also egi)—baby
jap-chae—stir-fried noodles and vegetables
ha jee ma—stop it (to children)
hakwon—educational institute, academy
kimchi—Korean hot pickles

mandu—dumpling
nuna—older sister
omoni—mother; affectionately, *o-ma*
ul jee ma—don't cry (to children)